# LET'S PRETEND

# LET'S PRETEND

*A Tale of Mind, Imagination, and Healing*

---

CHRISTIAN HAGESETH III

# DEDICATION

*To my sweet Laurel Anne*
*my best friend and proofreader*

*and*

*to my brothers and sisters who left Vietnam*
*but came home with unfinished business*

# EPIGRAPH

*"It is much more important to know what patient has the disease than what disease the patient has."*

—HIPPOCRATES

# TABLE OF
# CONTENTS

# CHAPTER 1
# HOLLY

WALKING ON A tropical beach, I don't know where I am or why I'm here. My memory fails to provide answers. I know the basics. My name is Peter Andresen. I'm a retired psychiatrist. I have two grown sons that are too busy. My wife, Annie, died in an accident several years ago. I have Parkinson's disease. I think I'm in my early sixties. I've been bankrupt and now I scrape by on a Social Security and VA benefits. I am alone and lonely.

There's nothing to do at the moment, so I walk. What's my destination? I haven't a clue. Lazy clouds loiter overhead while a ribbon of sandy beach stretches before me. It's low tide. My only companions are seagulls hanging in the breeze. There's not a person or dwelling in sight.

Ahead, I see something in the sand. I can't tell what it is. But, since I'm not in a hurry, I don't walk any faster. I'll get there in due time. The beach is as smooth as a billiard table. As I draw near, I discover the object is a stoppered wine bottle. I take it in my hand. It doesn't weigh much. Is it empty? There's no remnant of a label to suggest what it once contained. I carry it to drier patch of sand and sit down.

I've enjoyed wine all of my life, but not anymore. My nose stopped working a long time ago. It's the first thing to go haywire when Parkinson's disease makes its debut. On the other hand, if I can't appreciate wine's subtle nuances, I get by drinking cheaper wine.

Holding the bottle at arm's length, I feel like Hamlet addressing Yorick's skull. "Who are you and where are you from?"

Remembering long-ago carefree days, I answer. "Of course. Who else, but a bunch of young people on a party boat?"

As I wipe sand from the bottle's surface, I continue talking, "They corked it and threw it overboard to float aimlessly until discovered by an unsuspecting stranger. I bet the partiers put a message in the bottle."

I hold it to the sun and discover I'm right. It contains a rolled piece of paper about the size of a cigarette. Shaking the bottle, I watch the paper bounce around. When I stop shaking it, the paper continues to bounce. A full minute passes and it just keeps bouncing. Then I hear a faint voice coming from the bottle. Holding it next to my ear, the paper stops bouncing and I hear a small feminine voice saying, "Let me out, please."

I say, "Nah. This can't be the old genie in the bottle routine...or can it?" I rub the bottle. For some reason, I begin to feel uneasy. I look up and down the beach. It's still just me and the seagulls. Not a person or animal in sight. Why should I be concerned if anybody sees me? I don't know. Of course, I'm a little too old to believe in genies. But still . . .

"Go ahead," I say. " Do it." I pull the cork. Turning the bottle upside down, I shake it. The small piece of rolled paper falls onto the sand. Unrolling it, I read, "A little too old to believe in genies, you say?" It's written in fancy cursive.

This is starting to freak me out. I stumble to my feet and scan the beach. I feel a chill. Goose bumps rise on my arms. I step over the bottle as if it was a coiled snake. But then, I hesitate. Bending over, I grasp the bottle. Straightening my posture, I take the bottle under my arm and begin to march like a Marine recruit. When I walk like this, my Parkinson's shuffle disappears. Forced march. Hupp, one-two. Hupp, three four.

A drill instructor shouts in my ear, "Shake your ass, Marine." I stand taller and pull my shoulders back. "Double time, maggot." I was conditioned to obey without question. As my breathing intensifies, I feel stronger, more in control and lead with my chest.

If I'm not scared, why am I double-timing?

Again, the soft female voice comes from somewhere between my ears. "I really need you. Please stop."

Holding the bottle close to my mouth, I shout, "C'mon. Enough already."

I will not be intimidated. I will not stop. But, why not? I'm not on a mission. I'm not heading somewhere, am I? I pause and wonder, is "somewhere" anywhere around here?

Continuing to march, I arrive at a small inlet. I stop in my tracks when I see the most perfectly beautiful young woman and she's smiling at me. Melting, I feel like a seventh grade boy approaching the cute girl he has admired from afar.

Young, probably mid-twenties, she is petite and her smile is flawless. She's dressed in a black two-piece swimsuit. When she stands, I see her abdominal muscles outlined perfectly. A young athletic girl with a 'six-pack' just like women on *American Ninja Warrior*. My idea of beauty.

Entranced, I walk towards her. She waits for me and looks into my eyes. Not a hint of a sexual come-on. That doesn't bother me—I haven't been capable of sexual intimacy for five years. Parkinson's killed my ability to perform or even desire to perform. It's pretty nice to not get tangled in desire and fantasy. I recall Freud celebrating his loss of sexual desire. Sex changes things. It ruins too many friendships, not to mention marriages.

Facing one another, we don't hug. Instead we hold hands. I'm lost in her deep brown eyes. The hair of her brunette ponytail flutters with the breeze.

Usually, I'm a confident guy. But now? Nothing. I just stand and gaze at her...and wait.

Releasing my hands, she stands beside me and places her arm around my waist. I reciprocate, placing my arm over her shoulder.

Her voice soft, "Would you like to spend some time with me?"

Inside, my little Peter jumps up and down. *Say 'yes,' please say yes. If you don't, you'll regret it for the rest of your life.*

I stumble over my words, "Well...yes. I think so."

We continue gazing at each other for another long minute. My mind overflowing with questions. Her expression? Sweet, kind, but mischievous. With apparently nothing more to say, we start walking along the beach. As we do, she caresses my arm with her free hand and rests her head against my chest. Petite, she is the perfect size to fit under my arm. The last time when I was at my doctor's office, I checked my height. I'm five-seven. Twenty years ago, I was five-nine. We shrink with age. She must be five-four.

As we continue walking, I'm beginning to feel unsettled, but not afraid. It's as if I already know whatever happens will likely turn out okay.

"What are we doing here?"

She jabs me in the ribs. "Walking, silly."

I chuckle. Nice sound, chuckling. I don't chuckle much anymore. There was a time when I was a funny guy. I traveled the country prescribing the health-promoting benefits of laughter and positive humor to audiences large and small.

"Why do you call me, *Silly*?

"It's a term of endearment. If it offends you, I can choose another."

"It's okay...No harm, no foul."

I repeat my question, "I mean, what are we *really* doing here? I'm sixty-three years old, walking on a beach in I-don't-know-where with a beautiful, athletic young woman who appears to know me."

She stops and cocks her head to the side. "Do you want me to tell you what this is about?"

"Indeed, I do."

Her eyes darting back and forth, she looks like she is about to deliver a punch line. "Twenty years ago, when you agreed to get Parkinson's disease . . ."

THUD! What? Hearing those words...*agreed to get Parkinson's*, I become paralyzed. Deaf as well as dumb. Nah! This is bull-pucky! What's going on? Nothing's making sense. Everything freezes except her eyes.

As if searching an old musty attic, I scour my memory. Do I

vaguely remember something? She says I *chose* Parkinson's. How does she know I have Parkinson's? But of course, my pill-rolling right hand is pretty obvious.

She breaks the spell. "You know? I once was called to help a couple in their fifties. It was their thirtieth wedding anniversary. Same idea; they're alone on a beach and find a bottle in the sand. They rub it and I appear to grant them each a wish."

Is she about to tell me a story after what she just unloaded on me?

"And like all my clients, they were in utter disbelief."

I choke out, "*clients.*"

"Oh, of course, Peter. I'm sorry. I need to remember there is so much you aren't aware of...yet."

I stammer, "You know my name?"

"Of course. This isn't our first rodeo."

My knees become wobbly. "Let's stop and sit for a minute, I need to collect myself."

We seat ourselves on a pair of beach chairs—*Where the hell did they come from?*—at a small table covered with a white linen tablecloth on which I find an opened bottle of Batard-Montrachet, vintage 2000, and two crystal wine glasses. I pour the chilled wine into our glasses and take a sip. "Oh, that is nice, very nice. But it's way out of my price range."

My companion smiles as she reaches across the table and touches her glass to mine. "To imagination and the magic of your mind."

*What does she mean by that?* I take another taste, but I'm still rattled and confused. I need another minute to compose myself. I swish the wine in my glass and savor the bouquet. "Damn, this is one great wine."

I think back on my Parkinson's. It's been fifteen years (the best I can calculate) since I lost my sense of smell. Not a great loss in the grand scheme of things. If you have to live without one cranial nerve, losing your sense of smell causes the fewest problems. About ten years ago, I had a month-long ordeal of rock-hard constipation. Only years later did I learn it was an early sign of Parkinson's. It is called one of the "non-motor symptoms."

Eight years ago, my right thumb started to tap the beat of a different drummer. I first noticed it when stopped at a traffic light. Unwelcome observations by friends and family made it hard to deny; I was stooped-over and shuffled when I walked. My palsied right arm didn't swing, despite my hand doing the rhumba.

I feel kind eyes soothing my evident discomfort. I look back at my companion. "You know my name, but I don't know yours. What do you want me to call you?"

She leans across the table and plants a kiss on the tip of my nose. "Have fun, name me after someone you'd like to hang out with."

She's right. There were years when I was the life of the party. Besides teaching Health & Humor, I wrote a book on the positive use of humor for healing.

I remember a workshop I presented to a Parkinson's group thirty years ago. Persons with Parkinson's—we call them PWPs—caregivers, and medical providers. One man was, by all appearances, frozen. Almost no movement; his face chiseled from a block of salt. Only his eyes followed me, but he seemed attentive. I clowned my way through the seven stages of laughter. When it came to my telling everybody to make the craziest faces they could, he shattered his mask with a Cheshire Cat grin. Sobbing, his wife hugged him. Later she revealed he hadn't smiled for over a year. I heard from her six weeks later. She told me he passed away and expressed her gratitude that during the last weeks of his life they laughed together every day.

My companion brings me back. "I was telling you about an older married couple I worked with sometime back."

"You were?"

"Yeah, but I think you were still trying to figure out what's going on. Why don't you just let it go for a minute? You know, 'go with the flow.' Let me tell you about this couple. If you listen, you might begin to understand what *we* are doing here."

"Okay, I'll be quiet."

She assumes the persona of an Arabian genie (more threatening than pretty). "I met this couple who had been married for over thirty years. Each was to receive one wish."

She takes another sip of wine. "The woman spoke first, 'I want to spend the next year traveling around the world with my wonderful husband.'"

I tilt my head and nod. "Sounds like something I'd like to do."

"You'd think so. I gave the woman a folder containing all the documents needed for the two of them to take a year and travel around the world."

She pauses with a frown and takes an audible breath. "The guy took a while to say anything. Then he said, 'That sounds pretty romantic all right, but this is a rare opportunity for a man like me. So, I am sorry, my love, but my wish is to have a wife thirty years younger than me.'"

My petite friend stopped and smiled what, in the vernacular, is called a shit-eating grin. "I granted his wish, snapped my fingers, and he suddenly became ninety ears old. The whole nine yards, arthritis, half deaf, and a prostate as hard as a baseball."

After my laughter subsides, I look at her again. The scary genie is gone. In fact, she looks more like a young, athletic Audrey Hepburn.

"Which of her movies was your favorite?"

*How did she know I was thinking about Audrey Hepburn?*

She grins. "Sorry, when someone reads your mind, it can get pretty creepy."

"What is your name, really?"

"I don't have a name. It depends on who I'm with and what's in their mind; their emotional reaction to me."

I'm feeling a mixture of comfort and confusion. "You remind

me of Audrey Hepburn. And my favorite movie was *Breakfast at Tiffany's*. The name of the main character was Holly Golightly. She was whimsical and very beautiful."

"Is that what you want to name me?"

"Yes. Holly...Holly Golightly."

But my better mind cautions me to stop and think. "Holly Golightly's character was flakey and manipulative. You don't seem to be like that. I love the name, Holly. What last name feels right to you?"

"The word that best describes me is *Be*."

"I like that."

"Very well. From now on, my name will be Holly Be."

She points at me. "You need to go lightly as well. You need to get back in touch with your whimsical humor."

A funny story comes to mind. One I told at countless humor workshops.

"A man walked into a bar with a briefcase under his arm. Though he appeared wealthy (having arrived in a Ferrari), he also appeared depressed. He ordered a double scotch. Then he placed his brief case on the bar and opened it. A little man dressed in a tuxedo climbed out. Then the sad looking man took a small piano out and placed it on the bar. The little man seated himself on a little piano stool and started to play. He was excellent. He played classics, jazz, anything. The bartender stared in amazement.

'Hey, buddy, I've never seen anything like that. Where did you find him?'

"The depressed man wasn't enthusiastic. 'Well, it's like this. I was marooned on a desert island and about to die. I was digging in the sand for water when I happened upon this bottle. I brushed the sand off and a genie appeared. She said I had rescued her from her prison and she would grant me three wishes. Well, my first wish was to be rescued, and, as you can see, I'm here and I'm safe. Secondly, I asked for money, lots of it. And you can see I'm wealthy. But then, in my haste—or maybe the genie didn't hear me right—I made my third request. And now I'm stuck with this twelve inch pianist."

Holly bursts into laughter and punches my shoulder. "Now that's more what I had in mind."

And right away, another bawdy story comes to mind.

"Let me tell you another. I created this word, *gelastolalia*. It means if something strikes you funny, laugh with gusto. Don't hold your laughter in. Amplify it. The more willing you are to express your humor, the more delight you will experience.

"The concept of gelastolalia came to me as a result of having studied sex therapy. I went to Los Angeles where I took a workshop on the treatment of sexual dysfunctions. One concept we were taught was "erolalia." It means if you feel extreme pleasure while having sex, make sounds hat express your pleasure. Doing so will enhance your experience and your partner's as well.

"A couple in Southern California were having sex problems. In essence, the guy was a lousy lover. His wife took him to a sex therapist for training. Southern California is an interesting part of the country for many reasons. Among them, they have earthquakes. The tremors jolt or roll and can last from a couple seconds to over a minute. Their intensity is measured on the Richter Scale. Over five implies property damage; over six, the loss of life.

"Well, this couple went home to work on their erolalia assignment just as an earthquake measuring six point two on the Richter Scale hit. It was a 'roller' and it lasted for a minute and a half. Their bed began to roll back and forth across the room, smashing the furniture. Finally, it crashed out through the wall and onto the front lawn. The woman looked at her husband and said with satisfied smile, "Now that's what I had in mind."

I look at Holly. Obviously, she loves it. "You want one more?"

"Go on, you silly man. Hit me again."

Being a Norskie, I reach into my mental folder of Norwegian jokes.

"Helga and Herman were in their eighties, been married nearly sixty years. Herman was getting ready to die. Feeling no fear, he looked forward to dying. He was awaiting a sign from God. He had heard about the bright light you see when you're about to die. One night after he'd been up for a while, he returned to bed and shook Helga.

'Wake up, Helga. I yoost had a sign from God. I think I'm going to die soon.'

'For goodness sake, Herman, what is it this time?'

'Helga, it was a sign from God. I know it. I went into the bathroom. It was dark. I lifted the toilet lid, just like you always told me. As I did, the room was filled with a beautiful blue-white light. I put the lid down and the light went out. I lifted it again and it came back on. Helga, it was a miracle.

'Herman, come back to bed. You got your head crooked on your neck and you've been pissing in the refrigerator again.'"

Holly laughs so hard tears stream down her face.

She wipes her runny nose. "As our time together unfolds, stay in touch with your humor. Think of it a vitamin H."

I rotate my empty wine glass studying how the last drop has just enough volume to roll with each rotation. I put the glass down and notice the sun nearing the horizon; the clouds reflecting gold and orange. Minutes pass and the gold gives way to pink; the sun sinking below the horizon.

Holly is beautiful. I want to hold her, cuddle her, sleep with her. She just appeared from out of nowhere. And *voila*, I can dream of lying beside a beautiful woman again, caressing each other, and talking endlessly. But, there's no sexual desire.

Her musical voice calls me, "Hey, silly man. You look tired. Come lie down beside me and rest."

Holly gestures for me to join her on a double-wide sleeping bag. As we lie down, our legs naturally intertwine. Our lips touch ever so briefly and then I relax into sweet repose.

# CHAPTER 2
# INSANITY

E MERGING FROM SLUMBER, I wonder how many hours have
passed. I look up, but I don't see the moon. Having studied
celestial navigation, I look for familiar stars and planets. As I look
more intensely, a glob of mucus gathers in my throat. No planets.
Not a one. No Vega. No Alpha Centauri either. Clenching my
teeth, I can't believe what I'm seeing—or rather what I'm not seeing. There isn't even a Milky Way.

I try to roll over, but find I can't—my legs are still intertwined
with Holly's. I look at her naked body. Her breasts, perfectly
rounded, not large...not small. As I savor her beauty, she opens
her eyes.

"What's up, doc?"

"It's not what's 'up.' Rather, it's what is not up. The sky for
example."

We untangle our legs and I check to see if I'm naked too.
Nope, still wearing my cut-offs. I skootch to a sitting position, the
better to face Holly. "I don't know if I'm dreaming, psychotic,
or have arrived in some alternate dimension. I don't have a clue
what's happening or where I am."

Holly smiles while pulling her blanket around her shoulders.
Now the only skin I see is her face framed by her auburn hair.

I reach for my sleeping bag, but discover it is now a blanket.
"Where the blazes did this come from? Last night it was a sleeping bag."

I rub my eyes and notice the horizon is brighter. On Earth,
I would assume that direction would be called *east*. Who knows

what it's called here—wherever *'here'* is. I wrap the blanket around my shoulders as Holly hands me a cup of coffee.

"I understand you aren't much for tea, so here is your favorite coffee, Colombian."

Using both hands—an old habit from when I drank hot coffee on cold mornings —I settle my nose over the rising steam. *Ahh, so good.*

I quip, "I think vitamin C stands for caffeine."

Holly flashes a brief grin that fades. "Peter, I know you're full of questions. How would you like some answers?"

Until this moment, whenever I look at Holly, her beauty has been the focus of my attention. Not so this time. Now I focus on her furrowed brow and earnest face.

"Yeah, I want to know what's happening. Everything seems so unreal."

"I understand, but your situation requires special handling."

"My situation?"

Her hand shielding her eyes, she looks toward the rising sun. "First, let's share a bit of breakfast. Then we'll talk."

I turn away from the sun and find a Formica table right out of the Fifties set with melamine bowls of fresh fruit, a selection of croissants and yogurt. And, in case I run out, there's a steaming carafe of fresh coffee. We sit on chrome chairs with cracked seat cushions.

"Hmm, not up to yesterday's standards. I thought you could create a better eating establishment than this."

"I wanted something that would remind you of happy memories when you were young."

"Is there anything you don't know about me?"

"I know pretty much everything."

Back to breakfast, I slather my croissant with butter and currant jelly, then start to munch and chitchat about small things; like how sad it was when Buddy Holly died, or how we never liked Elvis that much. We're in agreement on one topic, October is the finest month of the year and autumn colors should linger a lot longer.

How interesting. I feel I've known Holly for years. I even feel a love for her growing; but not a touch of sexual desire.

"Is this heaven? It's not Iowa; that's for sure."

Holly laughs. "No, Peter, you're not dead and this is definitely not Iowa. I expect when our time together ends, your concept of heaven will have changed. But for now, let me say, human beings have made up their own versions of heaven. I'll let it go at that."

Finished with breakfast, we hold hands and return to the beach. Holly gestures for us to angle toward the incoming waves. "It's more fun when we splash our feet."

Despite playing aqua footsie, Holly speaks in a more authoritative voice. "Peter, I know you don't remember, but you and I had our first encounter twenty years ago. The setting was different and my appearance was also."

"Couldn't prove it by me. I don't recall a thing."

She drops my hand and pivots until we're standing face-to-face. "So you wonder what this is about. You are one of the rare human beings that has been selected to carry a message to thoughtful people. It will benefit many—not just those who have Parkinson's."

"What do you mean... I've been *selected*. Me? Peter Andresen?"

"Yes, you. Dr. Peter Erik Andresen. You don't know what a unique human being you are. You have been on our radar since the age of five when you first encountered insanity. You have weathered many devastating storms, yet you never lost your innate kindness or your desire to serve. Your kindheartedness isn't big and splashy. It's simple. And to us, the word, *simple*, is a high compliment."

I think back to when I was five and a memory crashes into my consciousness. But something is strange. While I'm looking in from the outside, a detached observer; at the same time, I am in the scene and experiencing every painful second.

My older siblings, Terry aged ten and Ingrid, twelve, sit beside me on wooden kitchen chairs we dragged into our living room. Three bare lightbulbs glare overhead—the better to keep five year old boys from falling asleep. We each have a stack of comic books to keep us occupied. I prefer Looney Tunes Comics—especially Bugs Bunny. Ingrid prefers love comics. Ick!

Tonight, our father is meeting the *Empire Builder*; the train bringing our mom home. She's been in the State Mental Hospital in Jamestown all summer. I visited her once. I remember two things: An old woman who walked up to me, pulled down her skirt, and peed on the floor. The other; when we met the woman doctor who was taking care of my mother. She asked me questions in a friendly way. But I couldn't answer; all I could do was turn away and giggle.

It's almost eleven PM when Terry shakes me awake. "Mom's here."

I feel scared but hopeful at the same time. I don't know what to expect.

Dad opens the front door. Standing slightly behind Mom, he tries to guide her into the living room. "Look, Catherine, the children stayed up for you."

Bleary-eyed, Mom looks at us. When her gaze settles on me, she screams, "What is Jimmy Santopolous doing here? Get that little shit-heel Greek bastard out of here! Get him out or I'll kill him!"

As she lunges for me, Dad tries to restrain her, but in the process he and Mom tumble onto the floor.

"Catherine, that's not Jimmy Santopolous, that's our son, Peter."

"No! It's that Greek shit-heel. Get him out of here. He's the reason I had all my trouble."

Mom looks drunk. Dad, lying on top of her, shouts at Terry, "Take Peter to the Berg's house. He'll have to spend a few days there. Catherine doesn't remember him. They say it's from her shock treatments."

A couple weeks later, Mom finally accepted me as her son and I returned to live at home. Yet, the following weeks were beyond difficult. Being alone with her for countless hours a day was the hardest. My dad, a traveling salesman, was back 'on the road.' Terry and Ingrid were lucky; they spent their weekdays at school. I was alone with Mom. She was lost in her mind, clicking her false teeth.

I didn't sleep in a real bed. My old crib was nearly large enough for me to stretch full-length. As those days churned, I remember gripping the crib's side bars and watching Mom stare.

A couple years earlier, she declared that being baby of the family, I must stay in my crib. She also insisted everybody call me *Baby*. A consequence of her calling me that was my family and friends stopped calling me Peter. Thereafter, my name was Baby Andresen. Not Babe like the famous baseball player...No! It was Baby, period.

As time passed, she improved. By Thanksgiving she returned to baking pies and cookies. Christmas was better, except Terry ruined Christmas for me. He told me Santa Claus wasn't real.

My mind clearing, I look at an aqua sky. A single word echoes in my mind. It's my voice, not Holly's. Loud and forceful, it screams, ENOUGH! I decided at the age of five, I will not allow myself to be crazy and angry like her. Instead, I will become patient and learn to wait in silence.'

The storm passed, my mind rests.

I wake later to find I'm lying on a blanket as Holly cradles my head in her lap "I think you changed in that moment. You developed the skill to look into your mind as an observer, and not react automatically to the events happening to you. That's when you first appeared on our radar."

"Is there a name for that?"

"Yes, it's called *mindsight*."

# CHAPTER 3
# APPENDIX

L YING OF THE sand side by side, we create our best renditions of snow angels minus the snow. Then we pass the time vaporizing small clouds drifting overhead. It's not magic. I've done it all my life. Though clouds blowing up and disappearing are normal meteorological events, I like to believe my mind has special powers enabling me to make it happen.

Holly hops to her feet. "Time to change the mood, Peter. Enough recollections for a while. Too many...not healthy. It can make a guy melancholy."

When she kneels beside me, I detect a mischievous twinkle in her eyes. I expect a caress or maybe even a kiss, but Holly has a different plan. Without warning, she picks me up and throws me over her shoulder as if I was as light as a feather pillow. I grunt as her shoulder grinds into my solar plexus.

"Careful," I squawk. Before I say more, she sprints towards the ocean. Not pausing at water's edge, she charges like a blitzing linebacker into the surf. When the first big wave crashes into us, she flings me from her shoulder and I splash into the water thirty feet away and sink.

Unprepared to go under, I snort an unwelcome snootful of water. At least it's warm and salty. I bob to the surface. But, before I can turn completely around, Holly pulls one of my legs and yanks me back under. This time, I avoid the snootful of water.

I gasp when I surface. "Lighten-up already, or I might have to get back at you."

I lie back and float where I sound like a camel sneezing clearing my sinuses one last time. Then I challenge her. "I've got a couple questions I'd like you to answer. What are you? How much do you weigh? Maybe a hundred pounds? You flipped me over your shoulder as if I was a bag of peanuts. What makes you so strong?"

She rolls over to float on her stomach and look at me. Interlacing her fingers beneath her chin, she says, "Aw, Peter, it's just more of my special powers. Soon, I'll tell you more about them. But right now, let's frolic."

"Frolic?"

"Yeah, frolic. Like you and I make like dolphins and make for the open water."

Now, I dig scuba diving. Snorkeling, not as much. But swimming freestyle into the deep blue. Nah, too much of a challenge.

Blowing out my sinuses for the umpteenth time, and remembering how my brother used to call me *snot bucket* I protest, "Nope, not this guy."

In a flash, she lunges at me and, again, forces me under. But this time when I surface, I've changed. I discover my arms are pectoral fins; my feet fused into a horizontal tail fin.

"C'mon, Peter, let's go."

She's off like a bank robber making her getaway from a heist. I follow as fast as I can and soon, I too, race along the ocean's surface, skipping from wave to wave. Giddy, I howl. As we undulate through the waves, we join a school of spinner dolphins—must be a hundred of them. Talk about choreography; they have no equal. All of us, real dolphins and make-believe dolphins, swim in tighter circles. Finally twisting into a cetaceous vortex. We merge into each other. No boundaries. Nothing separates us. I lose all sense of separation; we become one. Then my consciousness vaporizes like the clouds did before.

I awaken in a cabin to the sound of waves lazily lapping on the beach. Must be the cabin we saw earlier. I get out of bed and walk onto the porch. There I see two white chaise lounges with neatly folded beach towels. An assortment of fresh fruit, nuts, small sandwiches, and a full pitcher of lemonade await on a small round table. The goodies are topped off with generous servings of Tiramisu.

Holly joins me as I pour the lemonade. She has changed from her swimsuit into a light cotton sundress. She has brushed her hair so it frames her face; the ends just touching the tops of her shoulders. Coming beside me, she tucks her shoulder under my arm and out of the blue gives me a moist, soft lingering kiss.

I am surprised at two things: One, how moist, sensuous, and loving the kiss and, two, how I'm not aroused in the slightest. Holly doesn't move away. Instead, she sighs and hugs me a little tighter. "Doctor Andresen, something's not right. I'm feeling attracted to you. That's not supposed to happen."

Then, as if banishing the thought, she pulls away. "Let's sit and enjoy our brunch."

We sit and fill our plates. After a few bites, I say. "I could never imagine what we just experienced. Yet, it happened. It was real."

Appearing unsettled, Holly shifts her chair.

I see her discomfort. "I mean, swimming with the dolphins."

Holly exhales, "Think about this. If you couldn't have imagined it first, it would never have happened. Everything people have achieved was first imagined."

She pauses, giving me time to mull over what she said. "I think it's beginning to dawn on you we are in non-Newtonian reality."

"Whaaat!? Non-Newtonian reality?"

"Yes, a reality where physics doesn't limit our experience. A reality that is all mind. Notice I didn't say, 'in the mind' or 'of the mind.' You see, an *infinite mind* precedes life and material reality."

"*Infinite mind*?"

"A consciousness, an awareness, a presence unconfined by physical reality or time, capable of molding matter, originating and processing thought, and capable of instant communication throughout the universe."

"That's a mouthful. Give me a month and I might start to understand."

I sit back and close my eyes. To contain my racing thoughts, I practice square breathing: breathing in, count to five and hold for five. Exhaling, count to five and hold for five. Repeat the sequence ten times.

When I open my eyes, all I see is Holly's face. I peer into her eyes, perceiving a depth—a wisdom—I've not appreciated before. But, I'm puzzled too. I feel romance developing between us.

Holly continues, "Peter, you're a good man. Life holds more for you than you've ever imagined. I'm preparing experiences that will invite your imagination to venture where it never has before. When we were with the dolphins, our minds merged with each other and also with them."

I dwell on what she said. "All our minds—you, me, the spinners—melded into one mind?"

"Exactly."

"When something like that happens, I call it a *god thing*."

Ever the intuitive, Holly reads my mind. I mean...it's as if she sees the words printed out and actually reads them. "Peter, I notice you didn't capitalize the word, god."

I take a deep breath, stand, and walk to an upholstered love seat. Holly accompanies me as we sit facing each other.

"Holly, it's taken more than fifty years for me to formulate my understanding of god. Despite the craziness of my home growing up, my religious beliefs oriented me and comforted me while I was young. Being a Norwegian Lutheran, I wasn't given to intense emotional expression. Memorize the catechism, read a lot, and help the underprivileged. I read the whole Bible—including Leviticus, Numbers, and Deuteronomy—before I turned eighteen. I was *saved* while attending Bible Camp at thirteen. But I always experienced an inner restlessness. Much of my thinking about god started with the word, 'but.'"

Without warning, a memory crashes into my mind.

I am home at Christmas just before turning ten years old. During the five years since Mom returned from Jamestown, she had made several positive steps. Though prone to fits of anger and administering far too many spankings, she had gone back to cooking and baking and even participating in PTA. She reactivated her RN license and began working part-time at the hospital.

Of course, everything was far from being okay. Christmas, in particular, had a painful script that didn't change much from year to year. Some parts were good: lots of homemade baked goods; scores of Christmas cards coming and going; growing anticipation of opening presents. We kids always went to the movies on the afternoon of Christmas Eve. Mom stayed home baking a whole chicken and soaking a slab of fresh *lutefisk*. Dad did what salesmen were assigned to do on Christmas Eve, he delivered pints of whiskey to each of his local accounts. It was required, of course, he share the festive libation with each and every one of his clients.

One thing about Dad's drinking. It never caused us kids any problems. But it made Mom blow like Vesuvius. Dad was a happy, jolly drunk. Never angry, falling down, or profane. We kids rather liked him that way.

Every Christmas Eve afternoon at five o'clock Terry, Kate, and I would come home to good smells and Mom busy in the kitchen. We were responsible for picking up around the house and setting the table. About five-thirty Dad would walk in and Mom's volcano would erupt. "Chris, you've done it again. You've ruined Christmas for everyone, especially the children."

Well, I was one of those children, and it didn't bother me in the least.

Dad protested he wasn't *that drunk*. We kids agreed.

Nevertheless, Mom would increase the volume and profanity of her contempt. Ultimately collapsing on the kitchen floor and screaming at Dad. "You've done it again, you goddammed bastard, you've ruined Christmas for everyone."

Later, a variety of scenarios played out. Everything from my Dad stomping from the house and being gone for days, to a hasty, sullen truce and we all pretending nothing happened.

But this particular Christmas Eve had a new twist. Our parents decided our failed Christmas Eve gatherings were the fault of their three kids. When five o'clock arrived, we came home to an empty and very quiet house. Presents, normally under the tree, were nowhere to be seen. An hour later, Mom and Dad—both drunk as skunks staggered in the door. They took turns cursing us, telling us how bad we were, how we didn't deserve any Christmas presents.

If we tried to utter a word in our defense, they shouted at us, "Don't talk back." When we pushed it too far, Dad took off his belt—and for the first and only time in our lives—he administered a beating to each of us. Before Dad even hit Kate, she started crying. Terry tried to be tough and not make a sound. Big mistake! He didn't realize if you started crying, you'd only get hit a couple times more. I screamed with the first hit and got off with only three hits.

Punishment completed, they ordered us to bed without supper and told us if they heard any noise from us, there would be more belt action coming.

We shared a small upstairs room with a curtain down the middle to provide privacy for Kate. On our side of the curtain, Terry and I shared a three-quarter sized bed.

When we were young, Mom taught us how to say our prayers. Always fold your hands and shut your eyes. Lying in bed was okay. But, don't kneel by the bed! That's what Catholics do. Next, in a quiet but audible whisper, start with, *Now I lay me down to sleep.* Then the *Lord's Prayer* and finish with blessings on all of our relatives.

We didn't talk out loud that night. We withdrew into our thoughts and started a night of intense prayer. Usually, when I said my prayers, I stuck to the script and added nothing else. Except once when I was about four, I remember asking God to tune in Satan so I could administer him a tongue-lashing.

That night, I went all out. In Sunday school, they told us if you say a prayer and then add this specific phrase, "I pray this in Jesus' name, amen." If you do that to the letter, and do so with a pure heart, Jesus was *obligated* to answer your prayer exactly. No ifs, ands, or buts. Period. Guaranteed.

Another interesting fact about our family; everybody was expected to have their appendix removed. That Christmas eve, I was the only person in the family that still had one. The cool thing is, if you have surgery, everyone will be nice to you for almost two months. I recalled my fool-proof prayer instructions. I should be detailed in asking specifically what I want.

Here's what I prayed for: The third day of school when Christmas break was over, I want to wake up with appendicitis. By nine o'clock I want to be at the hospital and have my appendix removed. Mom and Dad would worry about me and then be very nice to me for at least two months.

Now, my parents never sustained their anger for more than a couple of days. They would return to their roles of cursing one another. Besides, two days after Christmas, my dad would be out on the road again. He was usually gone four nights a week. By New Years, I had forgotten the whole affair—including my impassioned prayer.

School restarted and we all fell back into our routines. On the exact Wednesday morning I had prayed about; the third day of school; I woke up feeling awful. My stomach hurt. I was nauseated. I had no energy at all. When Mom called us to get up, I remembered my prayer.

*Oh, no! I forgot to un-pray it.*

Quick as I could, I un-prayed it—Jesus name, the whole nine yards. Then, I waited to start feeling better. But, I didn't. My stomachache got a lot worse. When Mom looked at me entering the kitchen, she turned on her concerned-nurse mode.

"Peter, honey, what's the matter?"

"My stomach hurts...really bad."

"When did it start to hurt?"

"I dunno. I felt this way when I woke up."

"You're so pale." Touching my forehead, she added, "I think you have a fever."

In a jiffy, she took my temperature—it was 101. She probed my abdomen and located the tender spot, low on the right side. "Oh, dear! You have appendicitis."

I vomited a small amount of thin yellow fluid.

Mom was a whirlwind. Kate and Terry had left for school earlier. Dad was out of town. Within twenty minutes, Mom was in her white nursing uniform and we climbed into a cab to go to the hospital.

My memory is a little blurry about what happened after we got there.

I awoke from the anesthesia later that afternoon. It was already getting dark. Mom in her uniform, Dad in his gray suit, together with Kate and Terry, were gathered at my bedside. Just like I envisioned it in my prayer.

The open-drop ether anesthesia continued to make me vomit. The pain in my side was the worst I'd ever felt, but it went away when Mom gave me a hypo.

When I awakened again, a well-dressed man was with Mom. They had something that looked like a pregnant earthworm lying on a piece of gauze.

"Hello, Peter, I'm Dr. Ingalls. I took your appendix out. Your mother said you were a very bright little boy; you might even want to become a doctor. Well, this is your appendix. See the swollen area? That's where it was bursting. We call it a rupturing appendix. If your mother didn't get you to me in time, you could have died."

Even today, the doctor's words resound in my mind. The image of my rupturing appendix lingers.

# CHAPTER 4
# DIALOGUE

S INCE ARRIVING, I haven't looked around much. My attention has focused on Holly. We clean up after breakfast, then sit on the porch with our coffee. But, I'm am not settled this morning. Jumpy would be a better description.

*What's next?*

Reading my mind, Holly answers. "What do you say we stroll inland for a couple hours this morning?"

I don't answer right away. I continue to be preoccupied with my questions. Who is Holly? Is this place real? Why am I here? What am I to make of the tormented memories I have experienced? Not remembered—*experienced!* At the moment, I'm definitely not in the mood to go for a hike. Holly is a beautiful enigma. And here, in this unreal world, I'm convinced she alone can answer my questions.

"No hiking, not yet. I need to understand what's happening to me—to us— before doing anything else. For example, who are you? Or should I ask, what are you?"

Unfazed by my directness, Holly pours my second cup of coffee. "Peter, throughout history there are descriptions of otherworldly beings visiting humans. These visits are usually one-on-one events. Those visiting are called angels, spirits, or even genies; on the dark side, maybe demons or other malevolent spirits. Virtually all religions mention visitors somewhere in their sacred texts. That fact alone makes it clear any religion's angel or genie is a biased view based on the prevailing cultural beliefs and religion."

"While interesting, that isn't what I want to know."

Holly continues. "It, by which I mean the Universe, including all thought and consciousness, starts from the *infinite mind*. Sometimes when speaking about the infinite mind, we simply capitalize the word, Mind.

Seated in a full lotus, she faces me eye-to-eye. "The instant the Big Bang occurred, there was only Mind. In its first $10^{-43}$ seconds, the universe was very compact, less than a million billion billionth the size of a single atom. And it was all Mind. That Mind was and is conscious of itself. A Mind so complete, all minds and all consciousness were spawned from it. And the most difficult issue for humans to wrap their *finite* minds around is *Mind* is independent of what the Newtonian universe calls *time*."

I lean back with a sigh. I never expected a lecture on cosmology. "What does this have to do with me?"

Holly stands, walks to the porch railing and looks out at the ocean. After a contemplative interlude, she turns to me. "I know you may think this is too esoteric. But to understand what you and I are doing here; basic training is essential. And what I've said so far brings us to what human minds call God."

I think I'm catching her drift.

"The problem with *homo sapiens* is their mind is limited by their brain. Don't get me wrong, it's the finest brain in your section of the universe. But, it's shortcomings are numerous. It values material reality above the reality of Mind. When a *homo sapiens* encounters the infinite mind, they experience a life-altering, inexplicable event. A miracle, a revelation, a healing.

"Since their brains' processing is often limited to material reality, they come up with an explanation requiring a supernatural being. They want to cast their inexplainable experiences in concrete and claim ownership of their stories. Then they shun all other *non-believers*, convinced their experience is the whole nine yards."

I hold my hand up for her to stop. "I'm with you on this. I

want to know what this has to do with my being here. What's happening to me? With me? Now?"

I'm beginning to understand Holly possesses unimaginable knowledge and wisdom, yet she appears to be simply a gorgeous young woman.

She continues with what I hope will be answers to my myriad questions.

"Peter, let's talk about your appendix."

"Okay."

"What is your understanding about what happened?"

"Well, first of all, I didn't think about it for years...for decades. After completing med school, it took me ten years to get to psychiatry. First were the Gulf War years and the Marines. Can you imagine what it was like for a man who grew up being called *baby*, to climb into an A6 Intruder and scatter various forms of ordinance wherever he was directed?

"Then followed three years of emergency medicine; a time when I was on the front line between life and death. I characterized my experience during that time with an old baseball phrase, 'I won a few, I lost a few, and some got rained out.'

"My change of direction to studying the human condition came one night when I had completed a successful CPR on a young gunshot victim, only to find out my patient had shot his brains out. If his twisted mass of bloody hair hadn't been so clotted, I might have foregone the CPR. But I felt vindicated when I realized I had saved a set of young healthy organs for transplantation."

Leaning forward, Holly caresses my shoulder. "You have lived a very diverse life. Lots of opportunities to observe the complexities of what it is to be a human being. That is another reason you were selected."

"Psychiatry was meaningful, demanding, and exhausting. And it provided a way to study the human mind and pursue the origin and meaning of life. In addition, I observed the diverse interactions between mind and body."

Holly draws me back to her subject. "In retrospect, what effect do you think your appendix episode had on you? I mean your understanding of the mind and the role a god did—or did not—play."

"After my appendix event, I pursued prayer like a meth addict. But as years passed, I never came close to that experience again. I supported the prayerful efforts of my patients. But after a series of unfulfilling decades, I had to admit prayer does not have the results people claim. Of course, making that known to my *true believer* friends resulted first in my being the subject of their prayers. When I failed to return to the fold, many stopped trying."

"So that leaves you with your appendix episode. If no divine intervention, how do you explain the virtually flawless way it unfolded?"

"That has left me wondering. Do you have a take on it?"

"I do."

"Okay, I'm ready. Tell me."

"Peter, let's go for that stroll now. Enough digging for one morning."

I feel unsettled by her abrupt change of direction. "But I don't have any hiking boots or clothes. All I have is my shirt and cut-offs."

Holly sighs. "And I thought you were going to be an outstanding student. Haven't you learned anything over the past two days? Go inside the cabin. On the bed you'll find everything you need. Need I remind you again we are in a non-physical reality. Have you forgotten our time with the spinners already?"

I return to the cabin purposely mumbling, "Need I remind you?...No, you need not. Try shifting your reality mindset and see how easy it is...Not!"

I hear Holly's voice from outside my room. "Tsk, tsk, tsk."

I'm surprised when I discover what's on the bed. Lederhosen, a red and white checked shirt, green knee-high stockings, and a pair of well-worn hiking boots. All topped off with a green

Tyrolean hat. When finished, I look in the mirror. I like what I see. I tip my hat to the guy in the mirror. "*Guten Tag Herr.*"

Back on the porch, I meet Holly decked out in a dirndl with all the accessories. She curtsies. Her hair now tied in two tight braids. She takes my hand and, in a scene reminiscent of Dorothy and the yellow brick road, starts to sing the *Happy Wanderer Song.*

Holding hands, we skip our way up the path and over the crest of the hill behind the cabin. For me, it sounds like I'm in the Norman Luboff Choir; my voice, a full-throated baritone.

The unfolding panorama includes rolling green hills with a scattering of small lakes and a deep blue sky with only wispy cirrus clouds high above. The land is crisscrossed with footpaths. Songbirds are everywhere. They're adorned in a variety of colors, all singing as if they love the sound of their own voice. The Norman Luboff choir fades leaving only the birds filling our soundscape.

We stop skipping and slow to a leisurely stroll. This setting is very close to my idea of heaven.

"Holly, I've noticed you often don't stay on a subject very long before we head off on an adventure."

"Yeah, that's kind of how I operate. I know it can be distracting. But I'm allowed to go about your training any way I want. I think that play, lighthearted adventure, and humor fertilize your mind to deepen your understanding of Mind. If it isn't clear to you by now, you've been selected for post-graduate level training."

A wooden bench on the side of a pond invites us to sit a spell. An apple tree provides both shade and food. We sit and enjoy generous bites of our apples.

"So, I'm in training, is that right? Some sort of cosmic Ph.D.?"

"You could say that."

Before she can elaborate, I interrupt. "Let's tie up the case of my appendix. What am I to understand about it?"

"Well, my sweet guy, your appendix episode is an example of the infinite mind intervening on a personal level. True believers call events like that, miracles—something unexplainable by science or rational thought. For you, it took decades of faith, prayer, and study before you realized you had no ability to make your appendix event happen. You tried countless times, but never experienced a similar event. You came to accept your newfound reality and your previous religious convictions withered.

"This is the juncture where religions miss the mark. They tell their story over and over, and add similar stories. Then they string their stories together in a way that explains their version of the universe and what humans should do or avoid doing to gain favor with their God. Finally, they publish it, calling it holy scripture."

A long silence follows as I munch on what she said. Unsure what to say next, I stand and walk to the lake's edge. The water is as clear as glass. I observe scores of rainbow trout together with giant largemouth bass swimming among them. But that's not how it's supposed to be. Bass eat trout; they don't amiably swim with each other. Then, I remember this isn't Newtonian reality. I'm in the realm of infinite mind. Everything is possible, even though I seem unable to beg, persuade, or demand it to do my bidding.

"Whether prayer 'works' has nothing to do with how the person prays—or to whom. Yet the infinite mind, which we reduce to a mere personality by giving it a name, operates beyond our knowing. And it does so often enough for the careful observer to conclude something beyond human understanding does intervene in our lives."

Holly, now standing behind me, wraps her arms around my waist. "There, I knew you were going to be a good student. You have lived a life of enormous diversity and complexity, and you never settled for the *party line*; by which I mean any belief system claiming to know everything in the Universe, including the name, identity and thought of the infinite mind—calling it this god or that. And you came to that conclusion after fifty years of devoted soul searching, service, study, and prayer as a true believer. That, my dear Peter, is why we have met."

"Am I to conclude from what you've said, there might be a different course for my life when I return to my physical reality?"

"Yes, but what you share is up to you. The infinite mind does not require preaching or persuasion. I recall a wonderful quote attributed to St. Francis of Assisi, *Preach the gospel at all times. If necessary, use words.*"

"Will I look different? Talk different?"

"No, probably not. But, what will be different, is what humans call, *your vibe.*"

"Tell me more. I think I'm getting an inkling of where you're going."

Holly drops her arms and standing tippy-toe, plants another wet kiss right on my lips. "Do you remember falling in love. If I recall correctly, you said it was all-consuming—seeming to come out of nowhere."

An episode pops into my mind from when I was in the Marine Corps. "We hadn't yet deployed to Iraq. Our squadron held a party for its officers and their wives. Attendance was not optional. It was a time after the birth of my two sons; a time our marriage was lighthearted and caring. I had never thought about being with anybody else...ever. At least until a young lieutenant entered the room with his wife. One look at her and our primal attraction was powerful and instantaneous. Our eyes devoured each other. I felt an overwhelming desire to hold her and kiss her; to make love with her. Her husband and I introduced our spouses to each other. Fifteen minutes passed and we started to dance and became stuck like glue to each other's bodies. Electrical pulses traveled up and down my spine. I really didn't know a single thing about her. Yet the feelings in those moments seemed impossible to resist. I called it chemistry."

Holly and I both sigh deeply and then I continue. "It was nearly a year before we deployed to Iraq. Every party was the same. When we saw each other, the chemistry between us kicked in.

"It was obvious something was going on between us. My wife and I discussed the attraction numerous times and in great detail. It was obvious our sexual desire was overwhelming."

I pause to drink more water. My mouth feels as dry as a desert. "There was a time when she brought her infant daughter for a well-baby examination. It was all we could do to not give in to our desires. But, we didn't. We knew giving in to our passion would create enormous harm and change many lives forever. We said no formal goodbye. We never kissed. I called it chemistry—not love. In truth I didn't love her. I really didn't know her."

Holly asks, "Was that the only time in your life you felt this way?"

I shake my head. "Never anything as strong as this. And later on, I wasn't a faithful husband. My wife either. Later in our marriage, we both fooled ourselves that an *open marriage* experience would re-kindle our dry, empty marriage. But it did nothing of the sort. It convinced us our love had long-since withered."

My gut feels like I just swallowed a lump of bread dough.

Holly changes the subject. "Maybe it is time to let this go. I need some more fun time with you. Tell me a story."

"Before I do that," I say. "I notice we still don't dwell deeply on each subject that comes along. And that's okay with me. You might say, I've always been one who delved too deeply. Dotted every T and crossed every I."

I snicker at my intentional flip of the phrase.

Her lips down in an insincere grimace, she pokes my shoulder. "I want to smile and laugh with you, Silly Willy."

Dressed in my lederhosen, I bow, tip my hat and try to sound like Jay Leno. "Here, Holly, are five of my favorite one-liners:

"Have you ever thought if we tell people the brain is an app, they'll start using it?

"Or how about a line for old guys like me? I don't know how to act my age because I've never been this old before."

Holly grimaces again. Undeterred, I press on. "I miss the days when you could just push someone in the swimming pool without worrying about their cell phone."

I look up hoping for a faint smile. She remains stone-faced.

"Okay, Holly, here's one you should relate to: If aliens saw us walking our dogs and picking up their poop, who would they think's in charge?"

Finally, she smiles. Even better, her eyes twinkle as I deliver the last one. "Always follow your heart...but remember to bring your brain along."

I stand back, let my shoulders relax as we laugh together. "What's next, my angel-genie."

Holly responds with a deep throated cry that causes the ground beneath us to quiver.

Right away, I hear a response from across the lake. There, flying toward us, a great horned owl the size of a minivan.

"Whoa, would you take a look at that?"

The massive bird lowers its feathered talons and lands right in front of us.

Holly scampers onto its back. "Climb aboard, Peter. We're going home."

# CHAPTER 5
## GOD WORDS

THE NIGHT SKY, filled with a gazillion nameless stars has yet to reveal a moon. I'm not asleep. Truth be told, I'm not tired. Since arriving here—wherever *here* is—I've noticed I don't feel tired or sleepy. I'm either awake or asleep, nothing in between.

At the moment, I'm interested in learning more about Holly's world. Is it similar to the universe where I live? When Holly intervenes and we spin with dolphins or catch a ride on the back of a great horned owl; it's unlike anything I've ever imagined.

Lying together, our bodies entwined; it's just us and the silent sky. "Holly...you awake?"

"Yes, I'm here beside you."

"I've been thinking. I want to know what it's like to be you. Physically, you look human, but your mind is beyond my wildest imagination."

Gently tracing my lips with her finger, she says, "You're right, it's time for us to talk. What would you like to know first?"

I roll away and stretch; then rest my head on my arm. "Where do you come from? What is your life like? Were you born? Do you die? Do you have kids? Do you know what the future holds for humanity? Are you close to the infinite mind?"

"Whoa there, big fella. That's a lot of questions for a simple girl lying beside her favorite guy."

Her comment makes me brighten. "I'm your favorite guy? What does that mean? Are we like...going steady?"

She shakes her head and says, "Slow down. Take a big deep breath. Close your eyes. We'll talk later when it's morning."

Disappointed, I do as she says.

When I awaken, bright morning sunshine floods the room. I hear ocean breezes gently swishing the palms outside. Looking around, I discover I'm alone in the bedroom. Then I see a white sport coat, navy trousers and khaki mesh loafers on a chair. As I dress, I realize I haven't shaved since arriving. Seeing my reflection in the mirror, I realize I don't need a shave. Out of habit, I take a quick sniff of my armpits and stop when I detect the scent of gardenias. I wonder again if this is heaven. Before I venture onto the porch, I check my appearance one more time. *Not so bad for an old guy.*

Stepping onto the porch, I see Holly. By God, she's stunning! Her flowered yellow dress is cut perfectly, so an admirer can appreciate the curve of her breast. It's exposed enough to invite a glance, but not a touch. She sits beside a small table covered with a white linen tablecloth. Two sets of sterling silverware lie next to monogrammed napkins.

Holly shows me a bottle of Dom Perignon. "Vintage 1975. Care to join me?"

I'm wowed by the age of the Champagne. "Were you even born then?"

She throws her head back and laughs. "So, you want to get down to the nitty-gritty before we've even popped the Champagne?"

I ceremoniously kneel before her and bow my head. "Please forgive me, my lady. I come from a different universe. We humans often forget common courtesy. Please accept my apology."

Suppressing a giggle, she gestures for me to stand and draws me close. Wrapping her arms around my neck, she kisses me—a wet, open-mouthed kiss expressing blissful passion. "I love you, Peter."

What am I feeling? Confused? Happy? Yes, both of those and so many more.

I know I want time to stop. I return her kiss and add more passion, pulling her more tightly against my body. As I do, a strange awareness wells up inside of me. I feel immense tender loving-kindness, but not an iota of sexual desire. The last time I remember feeling that way, I was thirteen and had just kissed my first girlfriend. This kiss had the same effect. For me, sexual desire seems abstract and not particularly loving.

I carefully slow my breathing. "Holly, I had no idea love was in the cards for us. I'm not sure what love feels like without trying to consummate sexual intercourse."

Continuing our embrace, we draw back just enough to see each other's faces. Holly's knitted brow suggests something's not right. I wait while she briefly looks away.

She returns her gaze. "Peter, I've not had loving feelings like this ever before. I know it's not wrong for me to feel this way, but it's so unexpected."

I listen but have no idea what to say.

Scrunching her nose, she shifts into humor mode. "Why, Doctor Andresen, I think you smell like gardenias."

I laugh so hard; I fall on my butt. She pulls me to my feet. Brushing off my derriere, I take my seat. Holly does likewise and fills our glasses. We toast one another using only our eyes.

Enjoying my first sip of champagne, I feel more centered. "Now it's my turn to listen. I want to hear your story."

"A good place to begin is right here and now. I'm sure proclaiming my love for you might be destabilizing. Forget everything you ever thought you knew about my kind."

"And what exactly is your kind?"

"We are not supposed to feel and express love for our charges. However, the *Mind* wants us to experience empathy with them. We know when they return to their lives, big challenges and opportunities await them. AND they will not recall being here"

We touch glasses again. "You are destined to become an embodiment of kindness and understanding, sort of like a bodhisattva. During your tumultuous life, you've learned to release anger, negativity, and unforgiveness. Because you incorporated those lessons on your own, you were selected to move ahead with your primary purpose which is to become a healer—but one of a different sort."

I tip back my chair. My friend, Dom, counsels me to be cool, man.

Holly tilts back as well. "I am not composed of solid matter, or any matter for that matter." She winks.

"If I say I'm a spirit, that would be inaccurate. Humankind loves to name things. It's built into their brains. In fact, it is one of their brains' primary functions. But every time they use a name, what it represents is diminished. That's why I play with the term, genie. People get too heavenly serious when they use the word, angel. I think it's due to too many Renaissance artists."

She refills my glass and hands me a plate of cheese, crackers and grapes. As she puts the bottle on the table, I notice it is as full as when we popped the cork.

"I know you learned about Moses and the burning bush when you were in confirmation."

"Yeah, before I graduated high school, I had read two different translations of the Bible. Although I didn't dig the King James version so much."

Holly peers at the ocean again. Tilting her head, she seems to be listening to something I do not hear. A minute passes before she nods and looks back at me.

"Here is the *take home* lesson you need to understand. By using the word, *god*—or *God*—the infinite mind becomes represented by a few billion synapses in your brain. Every time you access that word, it is pared down in your mind to something smaller. And you lose touch with the *infinity* of infinite mind. *God* needs to be experienced, not dissected. Humanity has diminished an unde-finable, infinite experience to a word."

"That's a lot to wrap my mind around. But I think I'm begin-ning to understand. Humanity decided that the infinite mind needed to be represented in human form. God didn't create humankind in his image. Humankind designed God in its image."

"You've got the idea. Take Moses and the burning bush. It was written that God said his name was *I am that I am*. But what was first written down of that interchange, were four Hebrew characters, *yod-he-vav-he*; YHVH. It's called the Tetragrammaton."

She places a handful of sand on the table and then smoothes it out. Next, she traces four Hebrew letters for me on the table יהוה. She explains the letters she has drawn. "Each letter is a consonant, not a vowel. These letters were printed in a square the first time. Depending on the reading sequence, the characters can mean any one of the following phrases: I AM; I WAS; I WILL BE. The three conjugations of the Hebrew verb, *to be*. So, somewhere in that deep Hebrew wisdom was the declaration, the word we use for God—YHVH—is not a name, it's a verb, not a noun."

I'm glad the Dom Perignon supply is limitless. I pause for another glass and turn to look at the ocean. Now deep in thought, I too, slow my breathing. "Holly, what you're saying begs another question."

"And that would be?"

"Everything you've just said applies equally to your use of the word, *Mind*."

"Definitely. No doubt. You see, Peter, the physical sciences in the material world govern human existence. Before that first tick of time, the infinite mind already was. The physical universe was infinitesimally small. When the tick occurred, time became necessary for the laws of physics to apply. The infinite mind is not limited by time. You are limited by time, but I am not. Remember the tetragrammaton. It boils down to what we call God is not limited by time or the laws of physics. And we should not use a word for God more than a few times. If we do, the reality that the word is supposed to convey, shrinks and fails."

I stroke my whiskerless chin. "So, to truly understand the infinite mind, we should not use the same word over and over."

Holly beams at me. "But now, it's time for us to play. Enough heavy thought for this morning. Let's get down and start feeling groovy."

Something catches my eye; a helium balloon is floating on the sand next to the water's edge.

"C'mon, favorite guy. Let's go on an adventure."

We scamper to the balloon. It must be filled with Helium; I don't see a burner. No one is in the basket, so we crawl aboard. The second we do; the balloon rises and the wind blows us over the ocean.

How many times have I flown above the ocean? The answer, too numerous to count. Four years, a bombardier-navigator in the Marine Corps. I recall how we played tail-chase games among towering cumulus clouds and engaged in mock dog fights. And, of course, too many nights drinking more than any one liver should ever be asked to process. It didn't get stressful for me until August 1990. Saddam Hussein invaded Kuwait. Months before that, I had decided to say sayonara to the military. I'd had enough of serving my country. But my timing demanded something else. My squadron was ordered to have a role in the up-coming show.

Our plane, the A6A Intruder was really ugly, but carried a lot of bombs. In August 1990, my squadron, Marine All Weather Attack Squadron 224 (vma 224) settled into our new home at Shaikh-Isa Air Base, Bahrain. Peacetime flying was a hoot; dropping bombs, firing rockets, and navigating at night while flying five hundred miles an hour, a hundred feet above the ground.

Holly's quiet voice interrupts my mental meanderings. "Don't go there, Peter, not now. There will come a time when you'll need to go there. But not now. You're in a balloon, not an A6. And you're with your own devoted genie-angel."

Opening my arms, I invite her to come close. She responds with a full-frontal hug and a lingering kiss. "That's more like it. You tend to settle into melancholy too easily. Part of my job is to keep those times to a minimum. Remember, you're in training and you are my best-ever student."

Drifting along, our conveyance has a mind to follow the ribbon of beach. Nothing is hurried. I wonder if time exists here.

"Close your eyes, Peter, and listen."

A soft whirring surrounds me. I feel I'm in the center of a million tiny fans. The sound doesn't grow louder exactly, but gains intensity. I feel like I'm in the middle of a great living sphere.

Holly whispers, "Open your eyes and behold; you're flying in the center of a flock of hummingbirds—millions of them."

*Awesome* is a word used too often. It no longer conveys true sense of the extraordinary. But it is the only word to describe what I'm feeling. Every cell of my being is filled with awe. I bet Moses felt this way when he beheld the burning bush.

# CHAPTER 6
# BARNEY

BELOW-ZERO COLD AWAKENS me. I don't mean cool or raw. I mean colder-than-a-witch's-tit cold. I try to get my bearings, but don't have a clue where to start. I know I'm wedged in a tight sleeping bag inside a small snow-covered tent.

Where's Holly? The beach? Our cozy cabin? What the hell is going on?

I feel like a sardine in this mummy bag. Plus, it smells like last decade's mothballs. I haven't been this cold since North Dakota in the middle of February.

I struggle to extract my left arm so I can reach outside the tent and see what's nearby. It's too dark to see, but as I fumble, I sense a live body nearby. If it's Holly, I'd exit this igloo in a split second. Then I hear breathing. "Holly, is that you?"

What comes back isn't a voice, it's a deep-throated canine warning. It's not menacing; more like, "Don't disturb me." I've lived with dogs all my life. I know what different growls mean.

Damn! Where the hell is a flashlight? With my right hand, I feel around inside the mummy bag. Next to my armpit, I discover a flashlight. Forgetting the cold for a moment, I extrude my body from the bag. I click the flashlight on and look around. What do I see? A wad of brown fur.

I reach to touch it and discover it belongs to a German Shepherd lying with its back pressed against me. I wipe my eyes and look again.

*Could it be? It looks like Barney.*

I reach over and scratch an ear. As I do, a tail thumps.

"Barney, is that you?"

The dog stands and shakes. His alert brown eyes look me in the eye. "Yes, Peter, it's me."

I grab the enormous canine and pull him close. He responds by resting his paws on my shoulders. One kiss on my chin and then he leans back, gazing steadily into my eyes.

Barney and I shared some wonderful years a number of decades back. I had a hobby farm complete with dairy goats, sheep, horses, ducks, geese and a variety of colorful chickens. The hens' eggs were every color but white.

Barney's appearance was regal. Stately, reserved, ever-watchful, he was more imposing than Rin-Tin-Tin. I always could count on Barney to diagnose a problem and think how to handle it.

There was a time when our first nanny goat, Folly, was about to give birth. She went into the pole barn and laid claim to the open stall where all the critters usually gathered. She was nervous and kept trying to force the other goats to leave. Barney sized up the situation, vaulted the stall's fence, and herded the other animals out. He lay down beside Folly and, as she delivered her twins, he joined in washing each one. Not only that; he ate the membranes and the placentas for good measure. Satisfied he'd completed his work, he curled up beside Folly and remained there for the next week.

A year later we camped with two other families at the edge of a wilderness lake in Quebec. We were forty miles from the nearest phone. One of the children, Johnny, a four year old, wandered off. We didn't discover his absence until a half-hour later. Our group consisted of three couples and five youngsters aged three to nine. As soon as the boy's absence was discovered, we snapped into emergency mode. The women gathered the remaining children in the cabin. One dad headed to the lake. The other dad and I went to the road and searched in opposite directions. I walked, jogged and hollered for Johnny. Fifteen minutes, nothing. Then I realized Barney was nowhere to be seen. I whistled my shrill tight-mouthed whistle and shouted for Barney. Almost immediately, I heard Barney's bark; probably a few hundred yards into the forest.

I ran for two minutes, stopped and whistled again. Barney barked. We were nearer together and I was certain he was with Johnny. The third time I stopped and called, Barney emerged from the forest running as fast as he could.

I shouted, "Barney, I'm here It's okay! Go back to Johnny."

Barney spun around and ran back into the forest. A couple minutes more, I caught up again and saw him. He barked twice and ran on ahead. Then, when I stopped the next time, I could hear Johnny crying in the distance. "Go to him, Barney, I can hear him."

A couple minutes later, I entered a clearing where I beheld the most magnificent dog standing tall behind a little boy; his face covered with mosquitoes. Johnny cried. I cried. Barney beamed and strutted, knowing full-well he saved Johnny's life.

It's perfectly obvious why I'm delighted to find Barney. This time, I'm his *Johnny* and he's going to guide me out of this.

Looking in the tent, I find a parka, snow pants, wool gloves, long underwear and rubber overshoes. I dress and we start walking, but it's tough-going through knee-deep snow. Not to mention the wind-driven ice picks piercing my cheeks.

Despite our slow going, Barney and I forge ahead. When I fall behind, he returns to encourage me. I don't know how long this is going to take, but I'm not worried. I know Barney is in charge and is guiding me to safety.

A series of nearby threatening howls seizes my attention. Wolves! Damn! Now, I'm shivering from the cold *and* fear. Barney stops and looks back at me. "It's going to be okay, Peter, but stay close."

We trudge forward. The wolves fall silent. Further on, I see the sky is lightening enough to make out vague shapes and movement. I wish the wolves would make more noise so I could locate them by sound. Time creeps by. Then ahead of us, I see faint wolf shapes milling around. Barney stops and returns to me. I reach down, feeling the fur on his back. It's standing up. Despite my now-violent Parkinson's tremor, I can feel his deep rumbling growl. Though I can't see his face, I know his teeth are exposed and his eyes blazing. Another minute passes. I feel the wolves inching closer. Barney turns to face them while keeping his hip in constant contact with my thigh. His continuous baritone growl crescendos. One wolf steps forward, stopping an axe-handle away. Stiff-legged, Barney strides forward. Separated by a matter of inches, they glare at one another. Two gladiators entering combat will determine my fate.

With not a hint of warning, Barney lunges with cobra speed, grabbing the attacker's throat. He lifts the would-be assailant yanking its struggling body back and forth a dozen times and then throws the unmoving body to the ground.

I stop shivering; a fire in my chest bursts into flame. My shoulders relax. My breathing slows. My fear and cold have disappeared.

Chest out, head high, Barney approaches the pack. Submissive whining from the remaining wolves expresses their respect as they venture closer to Barney, but this time they offer him homage reserved for an Alpha. Ears back and tailed tucked between their legs, they touch noses one by one and then slink away. Barney returns to my side and like smoke disbursing, the wolves fade away.

We start moving again—faster now. I treasure my new-found warmth. While the sky isn't much lighter, I think I can see further ahead. The wind slows and trees are spaced further apart. I know Barny is taking me somewhere, but I don't have a clue where...or for what purpose.

An unusual sensation catches my attention. My Parkinson's tremor is gone. I'm steadier on my feet. I feel younger, a lot younger. Maybe the age when Barney and I shared our years together. I can't recall any Parkinson's symptoms since Barney made his stand.

The wind slows and overhead clouds are breaking up. A softer white light starts shining through. Then, for the first time since I arrived, I see the moon. It's funny how you take something for granted, but when it's not there, you really miss it. As the clouds breakup even more, I see the Big Dipper.

Could it be? Might I be back on Earth? Does that mean I'm back to physical reality? No more magic? I'm so confused. Then I reflect, feeling confused has become a habit.

Barney barks, getting my attention once more. He's further ahead. I think he's telling me to hurry up. I break into a jog and realize I haven't jogged since Parkinson's messed up my balance and coordination. Am I cured? No, more likely I've traveled back in time. I think I'm still in the imaginary world.

Damn, it feels good to run. Breathing deeply, I find the cold air doesn't trigger my asthma. I love it! Barney slows his pace so I can catch up.

"It's a beautiful night, Barn. I feel I've been here before."

He looks at me, smiling from ear-to-ear. His tail wags faster. Then he leaps forward inviting me to run alongside him. I do just that. Among life's most treasured moments are those spent with a faithful canine companion and simply being alive. I feel young and vital. Not old. Not shaky. I remember a line from a Thich Nhat Hanh meditation: *"Present Moment, Wonderful Moment.*"

Our path has been angling downhill. With the clouds clearing and the bright moonlight, I see we are in mountains. I'm unsure what time it is, but no matter. I believe it was Stephen Hawking who said, "Time is relative. Only the speed of light is constant."

I look at Barney saying, "That about sums it up, partner. What do you think?"

Stopping, he turns his head to the side and wags his tail harder. Then he resumes his trot.

"Yep, I guess that sums it up." I'm not sure which of us said that. No matter.

As I continue to jog in the knee-deep snow, my mind muses: Time and relativity...I remember Einstein joked, "When you are courting a nice girl, an hour seems like a second. When you sit on a red-hot cinder, a second seems like an hour. That's relativity." In this moment, I think that better than *courting a nice girl*, is *running with a great dog*.

We come to a rise and stop to survey the scene. Evergreen groves interspersed with Aspens. Several hundred yards away I see a meadow with a log cabin nestled on the far side; white smoke curling upward from its chimney.

Barney looks at me. "This is where I was supposed to bring you, Peter. The rest of the trip is up to you. You might learn, as I am here now, nothing really dies."

I fall on my knees to hold him tightly one last time. "Barney, you're the best. I guess we have to part. I'm so very sad to say goodbye again." I bawl from the deepest recesses of my soul. We parted the first time so many years ago when I moved to Southern California for my psychiatry residency—no place for a free-ranging farm dog like Barney. He moved on to take care of a deaf child who lived in the country. He spent his remaining years guarding and keeping the boy safe.

I prolong our hug, moving my cheek back and forth along his muzzle. Barney responds by washing my face with his tongue.

Then, responding to an unspoken signal, we part and Barney trots back the way we came. I head for the cabin. I can see firelight glowing through its windows.

# CHAPTER 7
# NORA

WALKING WITH CONFIDENT strides, I focus on the distant cabin. It reminds me of a Thomas Kinkade painting. Warm and inviting, the firelight in the windows suggests whoever's inside has created a special winter retreat. When I arrive, I first stroll around the cabin before stepping onto the porch. When I do, I discover there is no trail, no road, not even any footprints in the snow. Whoever lives here takes the concept of living-off-the-grid very seriously.

It's interesting, ever since Barney defeated the wolf, I feel restored, more vital. A threat to my life is gone. And I have no sign of Parkinson's. I walk onto the wind-drifted porch and knock. No response. I knock a second time, and then a third. Still quiet within.

"Hello, anybody home?" Same silence.

I grasp the doorknob and push the door open. The living space includes a kitchen, a dining room, and an open gathering area with generous seating; enough that a basketball team wouldn't be cramped for space. The final touch is a large stone fireplace filling the far wall. On top of the wood-fired kitchen range, I discover a loaf of fresh-baked bread and something simmering in a cast iron Dutch oven. I touch the still-warm bread and lift the kettle's lid. Inside, I find a meat and vegetable stew.

Looking around one more time, I call out, "Hello, anyone home? It's me, Peter Andresen. Are you expecting me?" More silence. But then I hear scratching noises coming from a bedroom. I open the door and out scramble two half-grown kittens.

They pay no attention to me, instead they tussle and chase each other around the room.

*At least I have company now. Too bad I'm allergic to cats.*

The bedroom looks like it's been prepared for a guest. A turned-down patchwork quilt exposes well-used flannel sheets. The bed is smaller than I'm used to, more like the bed Terry and I shared. A chamber pot stands in silent readiness at the foot of the bed. The floor is well-worn, but impeccably clean, linoleum. The room's only window is totally frosted over.

A mirror next to the door reflects my image. I look twenty-five years younger; full head of hair, no wrinkles around my eyes. I look at my body. Abs are flat. I touch them; they're tight. It's my body from a few decades ago. I stroke my fingers through my thick brown hair and just for the heck of it, I wink at my reflection. I check out the other bedroom—it's tidy and otherwise unremarkable. Still, nobody responds to my calls. Returning to the kitchen, I conclude it's just me and the kittens. I look outside where I see but one set of tracks, mine.

On the stove, scrumptious scents of winter cooking invite me to partake. Who is the cook? I haven't a clue. For whom the food intended? Me, I guess. When I look for a bowl, I find one already on the kitchen table. It appears to be set for a single guest.

I fill the bowl and cut a thick slice of bread. The butter, situated on the side of the stove, is nice and soft, the better to slather on the bread. Once seated, I find a glass of water, but I don't see any wine. I take my time eating. Mewing kittens rub against my leg telling me they're hungry, too. So, I dish several spoonfuls of stew into a small bowl. They love it.

The glass of water reminds me of my Aunt Nora. She only served water at her dinner table. She married an alcoholic who didn't know if you're a Norwegian farmer, you're supposed to spend your entire life working hard and not being shit-faced. In fact, the evening she died, her last words to me were, "Remember, Peter, life is hard. Work hard."

Her statement summarized her generation's approach to life;

immigrants in the eighteen-eighties, who settled in North Dakota, became farmers and raised big families. All the kids finished high school, spoke fluent English, and were confirmed in the Lutheran Church. When they became adults, their children followed in their footsteps. Nora never had a child of her own, but she raised three foster children. After her husband died, she was forced to leave their sharecropper's rental house. At fifty-nine, she went to work as a waitress in a small restaurant so she could earn enough to be eligible for social security. When she died in her nineties, she left three hundred dollars to each of her fourteen nieces and nephews. I never saw her angry, even when as a six-year-old, I dumped four dead blackbirds into her flour barrel she didn't discover until three days later.

Finished with my meal and feeling replenished, I notice the light comes from a few kerosene lanterns and the fireplace. I check out the kitchen drawers and cabinets, hoping to find some real coffee. Norwegians drink coffee at any hour; not even caffeine can keep them from falling asleep after a hard day's work. I'm surprised to find an open container of instant Nescafe. I settle for a cup and take a seat in front of the fireplace.

The kittens have had enough peace and quiet. I name one, the Roadrunner. The other, the Energizer Bunny. No place in the room or part my anatomy is off limits. They bounce from the back of the sofa to my lap to the table and to the floor.

It seems a long time since Barney and I made our excursion. I look out and I'm pleased to see the heavens have revolved several degrees around the pole star. Time is passing, but what time is it? Not a clue. Regardless, I'm tired and, whatever the time is, it's time for me to turn in.

I take off my clothes, especially the sweaty long underwear; then put on a set of flannel pajamas I found hanging over the back of a chair. I haven't worn a set of PJs like these since I left North Dakota. I leave the door to the living room slightly ajar; just enough for a little light to come in and allow the kittens to have the whole house for their playroom. Also, that way I can hear if somebody comes in while I'm asleep. Then, just like my ancestors, the minute my head hits the pillow, I'm gone.

I don't know what time it is when I awaken to the sound of a woman singing, *Oh, what a beautiful mornin'* from the musical *Oklahoma.* I immediately recognize the voice. It's Aunt Nora. She calls from the kitchen, "Time to get up, Peter. Get dressed. We've got a big day ahead of us."

I look around for my clothes, but they're nowhere in sight. Instead, I find the lederhosen I wore when Holly and I went for a flight on a ginormous owl. Looking out the unfrosted window, I discover summer arrived during the night.

"I'll be out in a second, Aunt Nora. Just gotta find my hiking boots."

She hollers back, "I put them on the porch when I arrived this morning. I wanted the sunshine to freshen them up for you."

Vintage Aunt Nora. Always looking for small ways to express kindness.

Standing in front of the mirror, I pause to admire my full head of hair one more time. My chin is as smooth as a ripe plum even though I don't recall the last time I shaved—must have been before this rodeo started. As I enter the kitchen, bright sunshine, kittens tussling, and the smell of bacon sizzling combine to create the perfect welcome.

"Good morning, Aunt Nora."

She glances up from mixing pancake batter and responds, a deadpan look on her face, "Oh, I see it's you there."

Her voice devoid of inflection; she continues to mix the batter. I burst into laughter. That dour greeting was one used by my Uncle Sigurd, a man who never had much good to say to anyone. Nora and I laid claim to that greeting long ago, while I was in my teens.

She beams at me, puts down her mixing bowl, and opens her arms for a hug. We embrace for a long time and as we let go, she says, "Look at you. How young you look! This time is sort of a do-over of the first time we met here. Must be twenty-five years ago. It was the first time you were exposed to the infinite mind."

She stops to wipe the steam from her glasses. "Today we will dig deeper. There is much for you to learn."

Looking through the open doorway, I gaze at the meadow and recall, "I know I have hiked here many times. Always thought this would be a good place to spread my ashes."

"It is indeed,"

"What was my first visit about?"

"The purpose and meaning of your life."

My stomach feels like I just swallowed two pounds of lutefisk. "Oh, is that all."

Nora goes on as if she hadn't just mentioned the most relevant question of human existence. "Peter, do you still like your eggs over-easy?"

"Over-medium. I got tired having the runny yolk stuff drip off my chin. My Parkinson's has made successful swallowing unpredictable."

"Oh, yes, your Parkinson's disease." As she flips the eggs, she adds, "It's a gift, you know."

"I've thought of it as a challenge, but never a gift."

As she places two eggs on my plate. "Last time, I told you *living a meaningful* life was the primary goal of life."

She returns the frying pan to the stove. "Ready for some bacon with your eggs?"

"I haven't eaten bacon in a coon's age. I'm trying to become a vegetarian."

Nora frowns as she places four strips of bacon on my plate. "Peter, you're living in the realm of imaginary reality at the moment." She chuckles, "We don't have to slaughter pigs here."

She takes her plate in one hand and a dish of fresh pancakes in the other. Without asking, she slides two pancakes onto my plate. Sitting down, she hands me a pitcher of maple syrup.

As good as this food looks and as happy as I am to be with

Nora, I realize I'm not hungry. I'm unsettled inside; like I have gas rumbling but none leaving. A sizeable fart might help.

"Aunt Nora, I'm sorry, but I don't feel like eating now. Something—I know not what—is rolling around inside of me. I feel I need to digest what you've said."

Out of the blue, I blurt, "Do you know Holly Be?"

Nora stops, a forkful of pancakes halfway to her mouth. She returns the fork to her plate. "Holly and I are your guides. We have the same task. Which of us works with you depends on what you need at any given moment. Right now, it's me; your faithful Aunt."

She continues, "Do you know each of us has been around since your mother was her most insane? Remember the kitchen knife?"

My most terrifying life event took place when I was thirteen. It was a hot July evening in Minot. Mom had just lost her nursing license because she stole morphine from her patients. I was told very little at the time. I didn't get the details until Terry and I were adults. At the time, Dad was still out of town a lot. But after Mom lost her license, he managed to make it home every evening. That night, as soon as he walked in the door, Mom shouted, "Iver, go out to the Friendly Tavern and buy me more beer. You know how it helps me belch and get the gas off my stomach."

Dad was unusually grouchy that evening and told her, "Get your ass off the couch and go buy your own goddamn beer." Adding, "My constipation is going to kill me someday."

Dad always put off his bowel time until he was finished for the day. Customers always came first; their needs took precedence over his bowels. Over the years, this resulted in a chronic constipation problem that required three or four enemas in a day, twice a week. With the only bathroom near Terry's and my bedroom, the stench of Dad's liquid enema discharge and his chain smoking, rendered our bedroom uninhabitable for a minimum of twelve hours. This meant I would spend the night in a sleeping bag on the front porch. Terry was working late at the drive-in theater; so it was Mom and me together, alone. Dad was never to be disturbed while in enema discharge mode. It was the law in our house.

I had found a way to protect myself from the household's black mood by listening to baseball games on the radio. Tonight, our home team, the Minot Mallards, was playing a Canadian team from Manitoba. Preoccupied, I paid no attention when Mom got off the couch and went to the kitchen. The game was tight. We were behind by one run; bottom of the eighth. There were runners on second and third with only one out, and our best hitter at the plate.

Mom shouted from the kitchen, "Peter, get in here right now. I need your help."

"In a minute, Mom. Yogi Giamarco's up."

"NOW, you little shitheel, or I'll give you the licking of your life."

Defiant, I responded, "Mom, I'm thirteen now. I won't let you hit me ever again."

Unfortunately, Yogi hit into a double play, so I got up from my chair. "Okay, Mom, I'm coming."

As I entered the kitchen, she sat on the floor, her legs spread far apart—I refused to look. What I did see was the hypodermic syringe in her hand.

"Be a good boy and help me with my shot. One day, you'll be a doctor and giving shots to everyone."

In the past, I had helped her mix her morphine syringes a number of times, but always refused to give her a shot. Of course, she lied to me about her 'shots' by saying they were cortisone for her headaches. Terry gave her a "hormone shot" once. After that, she never stopped begging him to do it again. She repeatedly announced Terry was going to grow up and become a gynecologist.

Holding my ground, I screamed, "Mom, I won't do it."

Then, without warning, something inside burst. I fled to the living room, hoping to catch the ninth inning. I shut out any sound coming from the kitchen. I thought I'd succeeded until I heard Mom scream behind me.

I glanced up to see her brandishing a ten inch butcher knife. "I'll show you once and for all, you little shitheel." I remember it was like the scene from *Psycho*.

I leapt to my feet and ran from the house. After that, everything went black.

Safe in the cabin, I wake up, drenched in sweat. I struggle to look around and realize I'm lying on the sofa.

Nora smiles at me. "I know that was hard on you, Peter. Fortunately, this is the last time you will have to re-experience those events. Going forward, you will *recall* but not *re-experience* these painful memories. It is one of the changes required for you to become a healer. Healed wounds create durable changes in your mind and in your brain. A wounded healer has the most to give."

As I listen, I feel something deeper going on. Something's changing deep inside. More than just words; her message is shifting my mindset. Imagine. . . never feeling sad or frightened when I look back over my life.

Nora stands. "Let's go out to the porch and enjoy the summer sun."

Once seated, we delight hearing birdsongs and winds rustling the trees. High above, two Redtail Hawks circle. They must have eaten their fill this morning. By late summer, their home is an empty nest. All they have to do today is glide on the wind and enjoy.

I tilt my chair and without warning, I morph into a Redtail. I don't think about it; it just happens. But I don't directly join them. Three makes a crowd. Since Annie died, I feel like I've been a lone Redtail. I'm used to it. But I no longer grieve. Yes, something has changed inside, and I like it. An hour passes before I return to the porch. I stretch my tired wings. I'm not used to flying alone. In the Marine Corps, I was the bombardier-navigator, the BN, not the pilot.

"Can I get you something?"

"How about a beer?"

Nora returns with a bottle of my favorite brown ale and a cold glass of water for herself. She draws her chair beside me and sits down. "Let me tell you more about how I understand the ultimate purpose of *your* life. You used to be a physician. From now on, you will be a healer."

"What's the difference?"

"A physician is educated in the science and workings of the brain and body. But they have little knowledge of the infinite mind. Many lack empathy and altruism. Too often they settle for the 'good life.' Wealth becomes their pole star."

"I don't agree. If I had focused more on accumulating wealth, I wouldn't be stuck where I am today. You must recall my last bout of depression. After not sleeping for a week, my judgment and my morals were scrambled. I made mistakes, costly mistakes, lethal mistakes."

I take another swallow of beer. "If I had accumulated some wealth, I wouldn't be broke today."

Nora shakes her head. "If you had focused on gaining wealth, you wouldn't be sitting with me today."

"But, people died because of my mistakes. I cheated on my wife. My second wife died in a freak biking accident. I'm alone. What woman wants a man who is incapable of sex and penniless to boot?"

I take another glug of beer.

Nora fixes me with her gaze, "Let me ask you a few questions."

"Okay, shoot."

"How many patients did you refuse to see because of their inability to pay?"

"None."

"How many patients did you charge as little as five dollars a visit?"

"A lot."

"How many lives did you save?"

"I don't know, but a lot of former patients say I saved their lives."

"How many suicides did you prevent?"

"Seven?"

"To be exact, the number is eleven."

"How diligently did you struggle to know God? Do His will? Seek His guidance? How many years did you pray and nothing happened? How many times did you go on medical missions to Third World countries?"

I don't answer. Her questions are rhetorical. She already knows the answers and I am uncomfortable with this positive talk about me.

"How can I be a healer when I have failed so many times and hurt scores of people?"

"Peter, saintliness is not a requirement to become a healer. Truth be told, there is no such thing as a saint. Qualities that draw our attention—I mean creatures like Holly and me—are empathy, a total rejection of hate, and a deep-seated intention to discover what is true—even if it means abandoning the beliefs of your childhood."

I take another swallow before I repeat a question that's been on my mind since I met Holly. "Who, or what, are you and Holly? Some sort of angels? Genies?"

"You're close. We exist in the realm of Mind. We are not made of matter. It may look to you like that, but we exist solely within your mind. Imagination is powerful beyond measure. But humans are not well-adapted to use imagination for their benefit.

For all they know, it's just like children playing a game of *Let's Pretend*."

"Are you born? Are you alive? Do you have a family? Do you die?"

"No. We constantly change, evolving to become what is needed by our charges. We are not born; we do not live or die in the human sense. But never doubt how real we are. We interact with humanity often enough that we have been depicted in art and described in stories since time began. I guess we are best described as helpers...guides. We exist so human beings might realize the nature of infinite mind and how to merge with it."

"If I realize the nature of this infinite mind will I change...evolve as well?"

"Yes."

"And I am to become a healer, which isn't the same as being a physician."

"Correct."

"As a healer, what will I actually do?"

"When you encounter a person who is wounded, it will become clear."

"Will I touch them in a special way, preach to them? Pray for them?"

Nora chuckles. "You won't perform magic or be an evangelist. Empathy and kindness are your primary tools."

"Will I be able to cure cancer?

"Wrong question. It's not you who does the healing, it's the *infinite mind*."

"Tell me more about this *infinite mind*. You've mentioned it several times. Holly has too."

"You will learn about that later. Right now, you need to understand healing. It happens via your mind, and it is almost as if the healing process is a transfusion from your mind to your patient's mind. Forget about total cures—they are rare and don't happen because of you."

Looking out I see it's near sunset. I realize a fresh understanding has been transfused into my mind.

"What's next?"

"I suggest we sleep on it. There is more for us to cover before you leave. But for now, you've had enough."

# CHAPTER 8
# DARKNESS

S INCE I ARRIVED, big changes often happen while I sleep. This morning, I was ready for something unexpected, but had no idea what it might be.

When I wake, gusting winds rattle the cabin. It's still dark. I look out and see a quarter moon. It provides enough light to see the aspen groves across the meadow have turned yellow.

High in the mountains, it's common to see the sky through a thin cloud layer, even while it is snowing. I recall this meadow being ten thousand feet above sea level. Despite the falling snow, I manage to see the sky and terrain pretty well.

Because it's still dark, I decide to catch a little more shuteye before sunrise. Before I drift off, I hear someone load wood into the kitchen stove.

"Time to get up and get going, Peter. We have a lot of work to do before daylight."

I light the lantern and look at the clock on the dresser. It's six-thirty. If this is September, the sky should lighten pretty soon. The bedroom is freezing, so I dress as fast as I can. When I enter the kitchen, I revel in the aroma of burning pine.

Nora seems distracted. "Get your coffee and take a seat, I'll have your food in a minute."

I've rarely seen Nora glum like this. I recall it happening when her foster son was killed in Vietnam. Throughout her life, she has been one of the most cheerful people I've known. I don't start the conversation. I know she will tell me what's on her mind when she's ready. The strengthening winds rattle the doors and windows. Still dark; no sign of morning. Nora's demeanor per-plexes me. During these days in imaginary reality, I've felt pro-tected—taken care of. Right now, not so much.

She brings my plate to the table.

"I know I seem different this morning and there is a reason. Today we visit a different domain of imagination, you might call the dark side. Humankind has conjured explanations of pain, death, or even simple misfortune by concluding it must be caused by an entity or entities that oppose the infinite mind. The devil, if you will."

She returns with her plate. "I'm sorry, Peter. This dark business is scary to my kind as well. Not because we feel threatened by an opposing dark entity. We know there is no such thing as a devil. Darkness troubles us because we witness atrocities caused by those who propagate ill-conceived dark beliefs. But let's enjoy our breakfast first."

Following her suggestion, we recall shared memories, not the looming darkness at hand. When I go to the bathroom, I check the clock. It's a quarter past eight and still its dark as pitch outside. Worse, wind gusts threaten to rip the roof from the cabin.

When I return, I see Nora's cleared the dishes and put them in a washtub to soak. She motions for me to join her by the fireplace.

"I'm sure you've noticed morning hasn't broken yet. There will be no sunlight today. Not until you understand evil is not incar-nate; it is a distortion created by human minds."

*Oh, just that . . .*

Nora tops off our coffee. "Peter, I know you've had diverse experiences relating to evil. Tell me about them.

"All right. I have studied the subject of evil—maybe too much. I first entertained the concept when I was five. Like young chil-dren around the world, I had come to understand death was real and terrifying. My parents taught me the prayer; *Now I lay me down to sleep.* Their intentions were good. They wanted me to be less afraid. The phrase that frightened me most was...*If I should die before I wake.* That put the fear of God in me—literally—and started my life quest to know and serve God. I wanted to be one of the good guys. I wanted to be on the winning team.

"Terry added to my fear by scaring me when it was dark, saying things like, *the devil's gonna get ya*. Once, I saw the devil standing next to my bed. I screamed so loud Dad came running to see what the problem was. I now know big brothers like to frighten little brothers. I also know he feared death and the devil just like me. In fact, at that time, the devil was more real to me than Jesus. I *felt* the devil's presence. When I sang *Jesus Loves Me*, he seemed weak.

"I remember one night that summer, Terry and I were in the alley behind our house. For weeks, we had been conjuring a scary devil-like character we called *the glowy man*. That night, I *saw* the glowy man running in the alley. I was terrified."

Nora pours more coffee and opens a package of powdered sugar donuts. "Please continue."

"During my senior year of college, I enrolled is an independent study with an Episcopalian priest from the department of religion. I picked the subject: *The nature of evil and the devil*.

"The priest responded, 'whew, that's a heavy subject. I'll be interested in what you find out.'"

I pause to organize my thoughts. They're like the tumult outside. I look out again to see if anything is different. What's different is greater blackness, no stars, no aspens across the meadow.

"Late on a Saturday night I was alone in the house I shared with three other guys. My housemates were gone for the weekend. After studying for five hours, I could no longer focus. Unable to keep my eyes open, I went to bed.

"One of my roommates was in ROTC and was the captain of its competitive pistol shooting team. Sometime, around oh-dark-thirty, I sensed a malignant presence next to my bed. It had no form, no color, but it was conscious. I knew it wanted to draw me in. It was cold like absolute zero. I felt it draw my life into its endless void. It was composed of nothing but evil. The only sound it made was icy breathing. I knew it meant me great harm. It wanted me dead. Specifically, it wanted me to take the handgun and shoot myself in the heart—not my head—my heart. And do it now.

"Then a new sound caught my attention. It was the sound of my roommate's handgun tumbling over and over in the top drawer of his dresser. It was calling me to come and do the deed—NOW!

"The struggle went on and on and on. I couldn't match its strength. I was physically and mentally depleted. I felt sure I was losing the battle until I found the strength to do one more thing—say one word. Only one utterance could make this terror stop. I tried to shout, but I couldn't. With my fading breath, I whispered one word. NO!

"Everything stopped...When I opened my eyes, I found myself standing in front of the roommate's dresser, AND I had opened the top drawer. I exhaled completely. As I inhaled, I picked up the weapon, removed the clip, and ejected the cartridge in the chamber. To be certain I would have more time if this happened again, I walked downstairs to the kitchen and placed it in the freezer."

Nora eyes me steadily. "Here is an important question: Just now, did you just *remember* this, or did you just *re-experience* it?"

I take a moment to compose my answer. "It must have been a memory. I'm not sweating. My heart isn't pounding. I just *remembered* it. I did not *feel* it."

I take a moment to stand and stretch. "I haven't recalled that experience for a very long time. I believe it was the most direct experience I've ever had with the embodiment of evil."

"What did you do next?"

"The following Monday, at the suggestion of my mentor, I went to a Christian psychologist at a local seminary and described my experience in detail. His judgment: I had encountered Satan himself.

'Go to your Bible and read only about love and the miracles of Jesus. Never get close to evil like this again. You may not come out alive the next time.'

I did as he said and quit my study, wrote a paper, and got a B for the course."

Nora and I stand at the same time and stretch.

"Let's take a break, Peter. How about we take a walk?"

"It's still dark and the wind is howling. But if you're game, count me in."

We bundle up and leave the cabin. Walking in knee-deep snow, I feel the wind isn't quite as punishing as I'd expected. When I look up though, I see the treetops being tossed back and forth. The wind makes it hard to hear, so we stroll side by side, but don't talk. Further on, the snowfall becomes lighter, allowing us to see the stars again—the yellow aspens, too.

From out of nowhere, a bolt of lightning strikes an ancient tree right in front of us. The following thunderclap is so strong it knocks me down. When I look for Nora, I see her standing upright as if nothing happened. I look back at the tree now engulfed in flames. Violent winds gather around the burning tree. They evolve into a tornado composed only of wind and fire

From somewhere in the dark, I hear Holly's voice.

"Peter, are you afraid?"

I scramble from the deep snow and see Nora is walking back to the cabin. I look for Holly. I don't see her, but I hear her again. "Peter, are you afraid?"

I look back at the still-flaming tree but don't experience fear. "No, I'm not afraid. Startled, yes. Afraid, no. Fear has lost its power over me."

I turn away from the fire tornado and make haste to rejoin Nora. I have a hunch we're not finished. I think there is more to come.

Once back in the cabin, I hang my clothes to dry. I return to the kitchen where I discover a bowl of fresh oranges. I peel one on my way to the fireplace. Nora joins me, peeling an orange of her own.

I'm aware it's deathly silent now.

"Where are the kittens?"

Nora chuckles. "I think they're waiting for the sun to come up. But it might be a while. You're not finished. You need to recall your most human encounter with *what-is-called-evil*. I think it occurred twenty-some years ago."

I lean back, close my eyes, and let the story emerge.

"It starts when I had been a psychiatrist for more than ten years. I had to work with the most difficult, most hopeless patients in our community. I made a conscious decision to enter the no-man's-land where psychiatry and religion overlap. I had no colleagues with whom I could talk. Then, a friend sent me a *New York Times* book review. The book was written by a psychiatrist who sought to integrate psychiatry and religion. W. Jon Millman's book, *The Path Avoided*, turned out to be a runaway bestseller. After devouring his book, I determined I had to meet him. I located his home in rural Virginia and wrote him. I asked to purchase four hours of consultation time to discuss our mutual interests.

"He was delighted to hear from me. He told me he would reserve a room in a guest lodge near his home. A month later, I arrived at his mansion in western Virginia and knocked on the door. A portly black woman greeted me and ushered me into Dr. Millman's study. His impressive library filled one wall. The other side was a fully stocked wet bar. Ten minutes later, he came in and introduced himself.

"I had scheduled two hours for the first afternoon and two hours for the next morning. We hit it off right away. Near the end of our time, I told him about my encounter with the gun-in-the-drawer incident and the warning I received from the Christian psychologist. His eyes lit up as he told me his next book was on the subject of evil. He handed me a rough draft and asked me to read it before I returned the next morning.

"It was deeply disturbing and, at the same time, fascinating. He envisioned the core issue of evil to be intentional deceit—telling lies. But what raised the hair on the back of my neck was his description of a"successful" exorcism. He believed some mental disorders were caused or complicated by a form of demon possession. That seemed too much for me. But what about the "spiritual" dimension? Such beliefs are part and parcel of almost every religion. Could he be on to something? I had said I wanted to go where wise shrinks fear to tread.

"That night I earnestly prayed for guidance. In the morning I decided I would become his associate. But above all, I promised myself to be an impartial observer. I would stick with the scientific method: observe, measure, repeat, make a hypothesis and then test. Stay with the psychiatry I've practiced. If something different comes from my experience, it won't be because I had already made up my mind.

"The following day I left Jon, a newly-minted apprentice exorcist with all the *fear and trembling* described by Soren Kierkegaard. I took on a task that might end my life.

"Jon and I regularly exchanged letters. Email wasn't around yet. He suggested titles for me to read and connected me with important people, including a Nobel Prize recipient. I was open to whatever came my way. We spoke about his one successful exorcism a couple times, but citing physician-patient confidentiality, he wasn't entirely forthcoming.

"His book about evil became another bestseller. The calls started coming in. He asked me to reply to inquiries from everything west of the Mississippi. Over the next few months, I kept careful records.

"His exorcism plans included contacting a protestant church near the subject's home. Catholics were always referred to their diocese. No Jews met the criteria for possession. The minister needed to be open to conducting the rite. Jon had an extensive list of such ministers because many had written him complimenting him for his courage to proceed with something out of the Dark Ages.

"After a year, I had detailed records on ten subjects. The information was enlightening. Nine of the ten were female. Eight of the nine came from Christian homes and had experienced sexual abuse as a child. Only one felt the exorcism improved her life six months later. Several entered traditional psychotherapy because of the trauma of the exorcism. During exorcisms, subjects were often restrained. The procedure often lasted two days during which the subject had no restful sleep. They endured physical confinement and never-ending praying in tongues. Two times, the"exorcist" went on to have sex with the subject.

"Armed with case studies, I insisted Jon hold a conference to report our findings to interested clergy and therapists. The meeting was held at a mountain retreat in North Carolina. About thirty persons—all men—attended. Evangelicals were most common, but there was a smattering of other denominations, including a Catholic priest and a Mormon bishop.

"In my opinion, the meeting was a success. It provided me the opportunity to express my conclusion there was no basis for a person to be suspected of demonic possession. I think half of the attendees got my message. On the last day of the meeting, participants broke into small groups for discussions. The Catholic priest went to the swimming pool to confirm baptisms and confessions of faith. The Evangelicals met to plot strategies about how to continue the war on the devil. The Mormon bishop left early. Jon got drunk imbibing a fifth of gin. Me? I went for a six mile run.

"The following week, I cut my ties with Jon. I concluded personifying evil is a maneuver used by human minds to control forces they can't understand. It was bull-pucky and I regret being involved in the whole dirty business.

Nora sits forward on her sofa. "You told your story well. It was a courageous thing you did. You have done much to counter thoughts of incarnate evil.'"

I close my eyes and take several deep breaths. When I reopen my eyes, bright sunlight floods the room. The door is wide open allowing a warm breeze to caress my cheeks. I look at the meadow where a herd of elk leisurely graze. The aspen grove is brilliant yellow. So many birds flying, singing...it's almost too much to take in.

Nora breaks the spell. " Take the rest of today off. We have one more matter to deal with tomorrow. But tonight? Let's just hang out and reminisce."

# CHAPTER 9
# SOLOMON

HAVING PURGED MY darkness, I sleep soundly and wake after sunrise. Looking outside, I'm pleased to see nothing appears different: same meadow, same aspen grove, same elk herd. I hear no sound from the kitchen which is a bit odd. Nora is usually in there by now; singing and cooking. I dress and go out to greet her. But no one is here except the kittens curled up and sleeping. The door is wide open letting sunlight dazzle the room.

"Nora, are you up yet?"

No answer.

I repeat in a louder voice, "Nora..."

Hearing nothing but songbirds, I check her bedroom. It's empty and her bed is made. I saunter outside and look around. No sign of her.

Bummer. I guess this means I'll have to brew coffee and prepare my breakfast. I go to open the refrigerator and find a note taped on the door.

"Dear Peter, today is your day. You can do anything you want. But pay attention to what comes into your awareness."

Hmm. I think I'll fix breakfast first. Ever since Parkinson's started messing with my brain, the harder I try to remember something, the more difficult it is. If I leave my mind alone and don't try too hard, the memory often emerges of its own free will.

I brew a pot of coffee, eat two oranges and a couple slices of toast topped with homemade chokecherry jam. I call the kittens and open a can of *Fancy Feast* gourmet cat food. That will satisfy them for a while. I take my coffee to the porch hoping to reconnect with the Redtail Hawks. It's early yet.

In the distance I see two Turkey Vultures gliding on an updraft. They are easy to identify because of the slight V shape of their wings. I've never thought highly of buzzards. I think they are ugly, but I know they have their place in the grand scheme. But I like my birds to be sporty like a Mazda Miata. After a while, I stop looking for the Redtails. I'll settle for any noble bird that fits into my imaginary world.

Not spotting a suitable flying companion, I go back inside and clean up. The bedroom clock shows half past nine. I've not played with the kittens. I want to change that. I look in my chest of drawers and find one threadbare handkerchief. I tear two strips of the faded cloth and return to the kitchen to find a roll of twine. I cut two lengths of twine and tie them to the cloth strips. *Voilà!* Two perfect toys to engage the kittens.

We start in the kitchen where I tease them into chasing and jumping at the cloth mice. After a couple trips around the inside of the cabin, I back onto the porch encouraging them to follow me and play outside. But I stop when I hear a low-pitched birdlike squawk behind me. The kittens want no part of whatever is making the sound and scramble back to the safety of the kitchen. I turn and see a raven perched on the porch railing. It's holding a shiny coin in its beak. The coin is about the size of a quarter and gold in color. The raven cocks it's head and jumps down onto the porch between my feet.

Not forgetting my manners, I greet the raven. "Hello. You are most welcome here. Did you bring me a gold doubloon?"

The visitor drops the coin and jumps back providing me room to stoop and pick it up. Examining it closely, I see it is indeed a doubloon minted in Mexico. It isn't too worn. I can read the date, 1796.

"You must be a very wealthy bird. What should I call you?"

"Please call me Solomon."

"Or Sol for short?"

"Gag me with a spoon, Peter. I'm not your Jewish uncle. I am of King Solomon's lineage."

I feel nothing is unusual about my talking to an English-speaking raven who claims to be a descendant of King Solomon.

"I apologize, Solomon. Are you the mentor I was told to expect today?"

"Indeed I am. As different as we appear, you and I share similar values. But first, let's fly around the neighborhood. Don your finest black feathers and enjoy the beauty and freedom of a raven's flight."

"I've flown with Redtail Hawks. Does a raven do anything differently?"

"Not really. Don't bother thinking about how to fly. Humans don't think about every step when they walk. Just spread your wings and jump."

I do as I'm told; I jump, spread my wings and suddenly I'm flying. That wasn't so hard, but I'm aware ravens don't glide as much as Redtails. I look at Solomon flying ahead and then at my body. We're identical. I never knew the change took place.

In the mountains, ravens usually don't fly very high. Theirs is a comfortable, more leisurely flight; sort of moseying along looking for carrion. But Solomon, I notice, is behaving more like a hawk. He's discovered a thermal that carries us ever higher. I follow in his slipstream. He's the flight leader and I'm his wingman. When we're about five thousand feet above the ground, he exits the thermal and we glide along, expending the least energy to maintain altitude. I close my eyes and realize there is an autopilot in my brain keeping me level. I wonder if ravens can sleep and fly at the same time?

"Hey, Solomon, I feel like I could take a nap up here."

"Ah, Peter, you forget we have predators like hawks, eagles, and owls. The worst is the Golden Eagle. I know this area well. At the moment there are no eagles around. But I'd keep a watchful eye nevertheless."

I catch up to fly beside Solomon. "Hey, Peter, want to try some aerobatics?"

"Ravens can do aerobatics!?"

"We don't do them often, but I thought you'd like a taste of what it feels like. Do you want to try?"

"Hell, yes. Marines don't try...they DO!"

"Let's go." He shouts and abruptly enters a sixty-degree dive.

I do the same while hollering. "Semper Fi, Skipper."

And do we get into aerobatics? Oh yeah! Loops, barrel rolls, aileron rolls, four-pointed rolls, Immelmanns, precision spins, inverted spins, and the most famous, Octo-Flugaron. Our craziness goes on for a half hour until we are too near the ground to try anything fancy.

"Peter, I spied a deer carcass. Want to grab a bite?"

"Yeah, I'm hungry."

We land next to the scattered remains of a Mule Deer. Like flying, I don't have to think about how to eat. A raven's beak is a very effective utensil. Humans don't make a practice eating carrion, but now \ I am a raven, this venison tastes like Beef Wellington. Once we've gorged ourselves, we perch on a nearby tree and preen our feathers.

"Well Peter was that exciting enough for you?"

"You bet your beak."

"Good. Now it's time we get down to some serious talk."

"Go ahead. I'm game for whatever."

"How familiar are you with King Solomon in the Bible?"

Easy topic for me to discuss; "He was thought to be the epitome of wisdom, but people unfamiliar with the whole story stop there. Later in life, he allowed other faiths to have a place in the Temple. That got him in a heap of trouble. When he died, his kingdom split in two: *Israel* and *Judah*. Those living in Judah became what we know as the Jewish people."

"Good."

"But what does this have to do with me?"

"You and King Solomon reached similar conclusions. You

both came to understand \ religious beliefs are not etched in stone. As you align with the infinite mind, you will abandon canonized religious beliefs. Of course, *true believers* will judge you harshly because of it."

"Yeah, that's already happened."

"The infinite mind is akin to *the ether* which was purported to be everywhere in the universe but basically undetectable. That commonly-accepted tenet of physics bit the bullet when Einstein published his *Theory of General Relativity*."

"I understand your thinking. But how is that important to my becoming a healer?"

"Because virtually all so-called healers attach themselves to specific religious beliefs and consider themselves necessary intermediaries for healing to happen. You, on the other hand, understand a consciousness—one we call infinite mind—existed the instant the universe came into being. When people name it God, they mistakenly believe they have a unique ability to curry God's favor to get special treatment. Most religions, with maybe the exception of Buddhism, claim a special connection—and thus the ability—to get God to treat them differently from those who don't believe the same way."

I turn away and consider what he's saying. When I look at Solomon again, I remember I'm talking with a bird, albeit a very intelligent one. And I remind myself I'm in an imaginary reality, but that doesn't preclude thoughtful discourse relating to the meaning of life and my place in it.

"I'm with you, Solomon, but your theological discourse feels too cerebral."

"Oh, dear. That's what my colleagues say, too. Let me briefly summarize. Healers are guides; they are not physicians. They do no healing themselves. They accept no payment. They don't advertise. They teach their followers to *rest* in the awareness of the infinite mind. Healing is not necessarily a process leading to a cure; it's often a matter of easing suffering. There are skills healers must possess including empathy, kindness, non-judgment and compassion."

Solomon spreads his wings. "I'll leave you with your thoughts for a while. Meet you back at the cabin."

As I watch him fly away, I realize there must be an inertial navigation system in my raven brain that will return me safely to the cabin.

I take time to commit each phrase to memory. Brain-weary, I need to rest. I do what Solomon suggested. I will rest in infinite mind. I will ask for nothing. Echoing the Beatles, I'll *Let it Be*.

Before I settle, my raven brain informs me I'm exposed to predators on this bare limb. If I'm going to tune in, I better do it in a safer place. Too bushy a tree could leave me exposed to pine martens. And ravens know better than to roost anywhere near the ground. I select a small branch near the top of a towering spruce. A place a pine marten can't reach, while providing enough cover to conceal my presence from avian predators.

Standing one-legged on my concealed branch, I preen my feathers till they lie in perfect alignment. I close my eyes joining the flow of the universal mind. It seems to be easier than meditating. My mind doesn't wander as much.

Hours pass as I sense a flowing warmth envelop me from head to toe, but it's not like a breeze. If there were such a thing as *the ether*, that is what being in its flow would feel like. I take care to simply BE and not think. I rest while remaining conscious. I have no sense of time passing. And then…it's over. And as if a postlude were needed, an old Christian hymn, *Breathe on Me, Breath of God,* plays in my mind.

I move to an exposed branch, spread my wings, and jump. I give no thought to navigation; it just happens and in no time at all I land on the porch railing next to Solomon.

"How was your time?"

"Peaceful."

"What did you do?"

"I did as you suggested; I rested in what I perceived to be a sort-of flow. I remained conscious and didn't try to make any-thing happen. When my time was over, I didn't feel anything special. I didn't feel I was anything special. But I was immensely peaceful."

"Good. Many try to make something—anything— happen. Often what happens is a projection of their minds. Rumi said it best in a poem:

> *The mystery does not get clearer by repeating the question.*
> *Nor is it bought with going to amazing places.*
> *Until You've kept your eyes and your wanting still for fifty years,*
> *\*You don't begin to cross over from confusion."\**

It's nearing sundown. I am tired and I know why. My raven iden-tity fades.

"Can we go inside? I'm feeling strange."

"Go to your bedroom, Peter. Change your clothes. When you come out we will finish our time together. There's one last item to cover."

As I enter the bedroom, I morph back into human form. I'm learning to experience these transitions more gracefully. I put on the clothes hanging on my chair. My reflection in the mirror is still me twenty years ago.

When I return to the main room, I'm greeted by a young Jew-ish man dressed in black trousers, a gray wool turtleneck, Nike running shoes and a Yarmulke colored like the LGBTQ flag.

"Hi, Peter. I decided to change into something more contem-porary. What do you think?"

I stammer, "W-well...I guess...umm..."

"It's me. Rebbi Sol."

I look him over. "I thought you didn't want to be called Sol. Do you prefer *rebbi* to *rabbi?*"

"Rabbi was for the olden days; back when I supposedly had

seven hundred wives and three hundred concubines. Needless to say, those numbers were grossly distorted by the Scribes. Can you imagine a life like that? Makes me shudder. Now, no. I want to be called Rebbi Sol; it's more informal. Being here today, I'm a Reform Rebbi and I play a mean guitar. Actually, I was really a Reform Rebbi back when I built The Temple. But the Orthodox community couldn't stand it—they wanted me dead. I was a very unpopular guy when I died."

I go to the fridge to grab a couple beers. After I pop the tabs, I follow Rebbi Sol to the porch.

We toast each other. Sol saying, "L'Chaim."

I respond, "Skol."

I look at the meadow and notice the elk are gone. We tilt back in our chairs and place our feet on the railing.

"You said we had one item yet to cover. What's it about?"

Sol answers while gazing at the meadow. "You chose to have Parkinson's disease on this porch about twenty years ago."

"Either Nora or Holly said that before, but never told me anything else."

"I believe it was Nora. You were young and horny back then. You might have missed the message if Holly delivered it."

"I guess I have to take your word for it. I don't remember anything like that."

"Yeah, when we meet people like you, we finish by erasing any memory of our meeting. Did you watch the *Men In Black* movies?"

"Yeah, loved 'em."

"Well, we don't have anything as technical as a Neuralyzer. In the universe of imagery, everything is a manifestation of mind."

"Neuralyzer?"

He takes a couple swallows of beer. "Yeah, An electro biomechanical neural transmitting zero synapse repositioner."

"Huh?"

"The gizmo *men in black* point at the eyes of those who need their memory erased."

"Sol, you've got an encyclopedic mind."

He chuckles. "Remember, back in Biblical times, they were right when they said I was wise."

I'm amused, but I want to get to the subject at hand. "How did I *decide* to have Parkinson's?"

"Look in my eyes."

When he snaps his fingers, I instantly remember everything from twenty years ago. It's like seeing a video, but being able to focus on a hundred different scenes simultaneously.

Sol shifts his chair legs back onto the floor and heads to the kitchen. He returns carrying a couple more brewskies and a bag of popcorn. "Whatcha see?"

"It's hard to sort them out."

"Focus your mind on Nora."

One video pops up.

"It's autumn. I came elk hunting and lost my way when a blizzard hit. Somehow I found myself nearing the cabin. I knew someone was there because all the windows reflected gold from a fireplace. I knocked on the door. When it opened, I saw my Aunt Nora. Before I could say a word, she said,"You look cold, Peter, I have venison stew cooking on the stove. Come in and get warm."

"Aunt Nora?"

"Well, not exactly. Though I look like her, I'm from another reality. But, I am here to talk with you."

As I watch the scene, I'm surprised at how easily I accepted what she said without question. This time I've been overflowing with questions.

Sol hands me the bag of popcorn. "You don't need to remember this word-for-word."

I feel bewildered, but oddly, I don't feel anxious.

"Nora said I had come through great difficulties in my life, but I hadn't succumbed to anger. She explained the universe of imagination and taught me about the infinite mind. She told me I would be visited again, sometime in the future to learn whether I might go on to achieve a status where I could provide great benefit to humankind. She added I needed to go through more challenges and not give up my belief that my life has real purpose."

I pause and down my beer. Sol doesn't say anything; he simply looks at me with a gentle buddha-like smile.

"She gave me options of a variety of infirmities, but said the best illness to develop true equanimity was Parkinson's disease. It wouldn't shorten my life, but it would progressively disable me. My later years wouldn't be very golden. But it would provide me the opportunity to use my mind to make remarkable changes to my Parkinson's and help others as well."

"What were your other options?" asked Sol.

"She said the alternative was a long and healthy life. But that kind of life would result in not pursuing a higher purpose. For example, I could be a scratch golfer and win a lot of tournaments."

Sol chuckles. "How would that be a problem? I know thousands of men who would give anything to achieve that."

"I want my life to be significant. I want it to count."

"Did Nora tell you even if you go ahead with Parkinson's, you still could fail to make a difference?"

"She did."

"And yet, you decided to proceed?"

"Yes."

Sol beams. "That's why you're here now. Final training before you return."

"So, I chose Parkinson's disease. I wonder what my future will hold."

Sol stands behind me. As he places his hands on my shoulders, he prays in Hebrew.

I don't understand a word, but I get the message loud and clear.

CHAPTER 10
# PLAY

I T'S STILL DARK when I wake up. Besides the wind in the trees, I hear gentle lapping of waves on the shore. I'm finally back in Holly's cabin. Is she here? I've missed her.

I don my swimming trunks and walk out, being careful to not make noise. I want to surprise her. Low, dark clouds fill the sky. The humidity must to be ninety percent. Lightning bolts flash over the ocean, but they're so far away the thunder is a low continuous rumble.

I walk up the trail behind the cabin and then return to stroll along the beach. Still no sign of Holly, but I'm certain she's nearby. When I return, a lightning bolt strikes; simultaneous thunder shakes the ground. I feel the sting of hard-driven raindrops, followed in seconds by a downpour. I rush back to the relative safety of the cabin.

I can tell the sun has risen, but the overcast smothers the sunshine. Since I came here, how many times I've stood in a doorway, looked out, and not had a clue what's coming next.

The storm diminishes as the rain slows to a drizzle, but the wind remains intense. After my recent flying jaunts, I wonder how difficult it would be to fly in these conditions. I wonder, that is, until I hear Holly shouting from overhead, "Peter, come kite surfing with me."

I strain to see her. When she calls a second time, I spot her soaring overhead, pulled behind a parachute. She twists, dives, recovers, and soars faster than any of my avian companions. Very impressive.

She glides to a smooth landing near shore where she unfastens her surfboard and rolls up her kite. Once on the beach, she drops everything and runs to me. Her intoxicating beauty fills my heart, and still arouses no desire. We kiss long and passionately. I love her. All my guides are important, but my connection with Holly is soul bonding.

She's wearing the same two-piece swimsuit she wore the day we met. Out of some strange curiosity, I look to see if her navel shows. It does. Thank god she doesn't look like Gidget from the old TV show. Back in my college days, my roommates and I got hooked watching old black and white TV shows. Gidget was never allowed to let her navel show. Holly is a lot sexier. While I've been unable to experience sexual lovemaking since Parkinson's had its way with me, I do appreciate her natural sensuality.

I shake my head. Why do memories like this surface? They interrupt my thought. What *is* important? Holly and I are together again.

The rain—now a mere sprinkle has soaked everything. We sit inside on the floor, but before we get really comfortable, Holly prepares a pitcher of Pina Coladas. She returns with our glasses and plops down to chatter. Holly wants a description of each event. It's clear she knows what happened to me. What she really wants to hear about is, how I felt, and more importantly, how I've changed.

"Let me think about that." I pause to arrange my thoughts. "This world of imaginary reality is as real as the material world, the one bound by the laws of physics and the like. Here in the realm of imagination, 'stuff" happens. And that 'stuff' changes material reality by first changing our minds, and then our brain's actual structure. That's how creativity works."

I take another moment to savor the taste of pineapple, coconut juice and Cuban Rum.

"Humans are not well adapted to taking advantage of what imagination can provide. They often denigrate imagination to be simple child's play; frivolous, fun, but devoid of meaning or substance.

"Getting down to the nitty-gritty of Parkinson's disease, for example, I have done well because I refused to believe drugs are our only tools. The truth is, they aren't. Hippocrates said, *It is far more important to know what person has the disease, than what disease the person has. The difference between patients is the content of their minds.*"

I stop again to play with the remnants of my Pina Colada. Holly remains silent as I reflect more deeply. Then I look up and take a deep breath

"I have settled, once and for all, the nagging uncertainty I've had about evil. It is not incarnate—not an entity. It represents a collective attempt of countless generations of human minds to explain why so-called *evil* events happen or why people choose to manifest the evil contents of their minds. The concept of evil is like a parasite; it lives because it feeds on thoughts being directed against it."

Holly takes my hand as we stand. "Dear sweet, Peter, you've always tended to think deeply. While thinking deeply is critical, you still need to maintain balance with fun, humor, and play. It's time I take you kite surfing. The rain's let up and the sun is poking through. Let's go."

Among the many things I love about Holly, her child-like pursuit of fun is tops. We walk to the beach where she dropped her gear. But now there are two piles.

"Okay, Peter, let me show you what to do. Here is your wetsuit, a bidirectional surfboard, lines and harness, a directional control device, and an inflatable kite."

"Whoa, girl. Remember I have a hard time tying my shoes. How do you expect me to get all that gear on the right way?"

"When you return material reality, I doubt kite-surfing will be in your playbook, so let me take care of this. Stand still with your arms out and your eyes closed. When I say it's okay, open your eyes."

Eyes closed, I feel a dervish swirling around me and then Holly says, "Okay." When I do, I'm astride the surfboard a hundred feet from shore and ready to rock and roll.

"Now remember, just picture yourself kitesurfing and everything will take care of itself."

"That might work, if I'd ever watched someone do it. Seeing you this morning was my first time."

Holly exhales like a disgusted step-mother, pretending she's upset with my lack of understanding. "The power comes when your kite catches air. You direct the kite with your control bar. You use the board anytime it touches the water. What's hard about that?"

"I guess I'm a little daft. Can you show me how you do it?"

"Peter, do you really have to ask? You've been flying with Red-tail Hawks and Ravens. Did you ask them questions like this?"

"No."

"You know what's happening to you, don't you? Your mindset is stuck. Shift it!"

Taking a deep breath, I jump like Solomon showed me, and just like that, I'm airborne. Without trying to figure anything out, I roll to my left and complete a perfect barrel roll, just like in the A-6. And then, I go through all the aerobatics just as I had with Solomon.

*Where's Holly?*

"I'm at your six, Marine. Show me what you've got. See if you can shake me."

She zips past me and I follow. I give it all I've got and more. We gotta be flying close to six hundred miles an hour. The clouds mass has been reduced by the storm; now they're simple tall cumulous clouds, just like ice cream castles in the air...and I remember Joni Mitchell's song

Ahh, the unfettered mind is a great place to hang out. That is . . .

Until I'm stunned by a deafening BOOM. Something or

someone just broke the sound barrier right beside me. I shake my head. Of course, it's Holly with her afterburners flaming.

I don't switch on my afterburners. Instead, I glide to the water and start a leisurely giant slalom. Not long after, Holly buzzes me and then returns to come alongside.

"Peter, how come you didn't go supersonic?"

"I think I turned chicken. Let's think about heading back."

"No, not yet. I saw a pod of Orcas. Let's go play with them."

"All-righty then; sounds exciting. Let's do it."

We become airborne in seconds. Holly goes full-throttle again.

*Does she ever do anything at normal speed?*

Zooming along, five hundred feet above the water, we close on the pod and slow to match their speed.

Holly approaches the leader until her face is a foot from his eye. The whale rolls on its side to see Holly's eye. Next I hear a series of whistles and clicks coming from the orca. Holly responds in kind.

"Are you talking with that whale?"

"Yeah. He says they're on their way to feast on a dead humpback. He wants to know if we want to join them."

"Nah, I've eaten whale before. One time is enough."

"You ate blubber?"

"Yuk, no. I had its muscle meat. It's dark red and tastes like liver."

Holly pulls away from the whale and glides beside me. "Where did you eat it?"

"Tromsø, Norway. That's where my grandparents came from."

"Peter, I declare, you're the first person I've ever met who's eaten whale meat."

"Well, Holly, I declare you're the first genie I've met who talks with whales."

With that, we peel off from the whale pod and return home. Once there, we change into more comfortable clothes. Holly dons the yellow dress she wore last week. I dress in loose-fitting black yoga pants and an olive-green T-shirt with USMC emblazoned across the chest.

"Can I fix you something, Peter?"

"Maybe something simple like a PB & J, potato chips, and a Pepsi. No need for wine or a sweet dessert."

It's late afternoon and peaceful, there's hardly a trace left from the morning's storm. We munch on our simple fixins. The temperature and humidity are perfect. I flip my hand back and forth and sense neither coolness nor warmth.

"Look, the air temperature and humidity are in perfect sync."

Holly returns with more vittles and sits on the floor facing me. "It's time we talk about sex."

*I did not see that coming.*

"This morning you were thinking how much you enjoyed seeing my navel as opposed to Gidget's navel being hidden by her swimsuit."

At first, I don't respond. Instead, I get up, walk to the porch and look out at the water. I feel like something alive is coiling in my gut; I'm not sure what it is. Then, memories flood my consciousness. It feels like I'm about to lance a boil to purge the pus.

I start a monolog.

"How ignorant was I at seven years old? With regard to sexuality, I was an idiot. No one ever told me how babies are born. I thought boy babies came from fathers and girl babies from mothers. Seemed logical to me. Terry told me I was wrong. I didn't believe him until my parents confirmed only women have babies. No further explanation was offered.

"At thirteen, I experienced my first orgasm. I had been having erections during the previous year when, one day, something inside me urged me to hump a rolled up blanket. Next thing I knew—the most incredible, warm, throbbing flow started in my penis and filled my entire body. Ecstasy. When it was over, I experienced immediate guilt and shame. *I will never do this again. It's sinful for sure.*

"The first time I saw a vagina was at a strip show during the

North Dakota State Fair. I was eighteen; just graduated from high school. How did that happen? I mean, how did I live for eighteen years and never see a woman's privates?

"My first intercourse occurred at twenty-two. My girlfriend and I were both first-timers. It was uncomfortable for both of us and hard to achieve orgasm. Our experience was better the next two times, but my girlfriend freaked out when we got together the fourth time. Hyperventilating and crying uncontrollably, she pushed me away. "I never want to lay eyes on you again, you bastard." Looking back with my psychiatric training, I think she was a victim of sexual abuse.

"A year later my next girlfriend said she was taking birth control pills. Finally, I had a relationship that provided freedom of sexual expression—a lot of screwing. Two months later she announced she was pregnant. She hadn't taken the birth control pills consistently. She explained she was promiscuous in high school and thought she couldn't get pregnant. That was a tragic outcome for us. She had an abortion and we broke up."

Holly now standing behind me hugs me like she'll never let go. "Time after time, despite what has happened to you, you don't resort to anger, fear, or self-pity. It's like Yoda said, *Fear is the path to the dark side. Fear leads to anger; anger leads to hate; hate leads to suffering.*"

I turn to face her to continue our embrace. Holly's heart beats so hard, I can feel it. I place my finger on her chest. "I don't remember that happening before."

I get lost in her brown eyes. They remind me of the song, *Drink to me with only thine eyes and I will pledge with mine.*

Holly's eyes start dancing back and forth as she mockingly pleads, "Does that mean we won't toast each other with wine, too?"

I chuckle. "I've been waiting for you to bring that up."

"What would you like?"

"A good Bordeaux, like a 1996 Mouton Rothschild."

She winks. "That's a five hundred dollar bottle; the best France has to offer at the moment. Good choice, Boyfriend."

We sit on a pair of deck chairs and linger over the finest wine I've ever tasted. When I place my glass on the table between us, I discover five different kinds of cheese, a selection of different crackers, and a small bowl of caviar.

"You have the magic touch, Girlfriend."

"Anything to please you, Silly Man."

"I like it when you call me, 'Silly Man'. It's friendly teasing. I know how you really feel about me."

She pretends to mock me. "And that is...?"

"I think you feel like my Uncle Sigurd would say, 'not half bad.'"

"Truth be known, I want to spend the rest of your Earth-life with you."

"But, that's not allowed, right?"

"No, but I'll find out if there's any way around it. This has never come up for me or anyone I know."

This time I'm the one who bounces up. "What do you say we go skinny dipping?"

"You've got a deal."

In a split second we're naked and running into the water, where we swim like humans for a change. It's a leisurely freestyle at first, but soon we switch to side stroke so we can see each other's bodies. As I look at her, I have no interest in her navel or her vagina. Her breasts are works of art, but I am not inclined to touch them.

She gestures for us to stop and tread water. "Here is my thinking about sexuality. Life requires strong incentives to procreate. That has been accomplished by creating an ecstatic feeling when copulating. Early on, humans had serial intimate partners. But when a woman became pregnant, a deeper drive developed. They stayed together until the baby was no longer breastfeeding and the woman could conceive again. At that time, they often found a different mate. That process worked until agriculture came along and people settled down in one place. That also marked the beginning of organized religion. Each religion codified a set of mores defining behaviors, punishments, and judgments—especially those relating to sexual conduct. Celibacy was a misguided attempt to subdue sexual desire, preferring a life with no copulation to achieve a loftier goal. The current state of the Catholic priests hasn't worked out so well. In fact, there are scant Biblical references to support celibacy. But in the twelfth century, a new rule came into being: priests had to be celibate."

Holly stops to take a breath.

"You know, Holly, you're a virtual Wikipedia; you're not just another pretty face. Let's go back to the cabin and get lazy."

We race back. I think Holly slows a little to urge me to swim faster, but she still makes it back before me. I watch her walk up the beach and again appreciate how beautiful her nude body is.

She slows, giving me time to catch up. When I do, she turns to press her body into mine. We move as if we're slow dancing. I love the feeling of our bodies touching and caressing each other.

"Peter, you're one of a kind. It's not all me. I've never experienced love like this before. Why now? Why you?"

I get lost in her eyes again. "I have no answers."

We soften our embrace and step back to admire each other's body.

"Peter, how do you prefer to see me? Like this? Or with clothes on?"

"I like both, but most of the time, I prefer you wear attractive clothing. Tasteful clothing is like a frame around a beautiful painting."

My beaming Holly walks into the cabin. "Let's get dressed. There's one more matter to discuss."

I dawdle a bit. I don't want to hurry anything. When I return to the porch, Holly is wearing a grass skirt, a tank-top, and a single gardenia in her hair. Since eating together is one of our delightful customs, she has prepared a table with every fruit imaginable.

"You said there was one more matter for us to discuss."

"Yeah, it's your sexuality or lack thereof."

"What are you getting at?"

"When you chose Parkinson's disease, did you think it would mean the end of sexual experience as you knew it?"

"No. When people think about Parkinson's they only think about tremor and rigidity. I had to read more about the loss of sexual mojo after it happened to me. It's more common than I thought, but it isn't universal."

"Here in imaginary reality, we decided it would be better for you to be like a eunuch when you became a healer. It will free you to focus on your patients. It's like Kierkegaard said, *Purity of heart is to will one thing.* When you go back, your most important asset will be your pure heart."

"I think my lack of sexual desire is a blessing."

"It is. Now you need to learn more about what a healer actually does."

# CHAPTER 11
## THE COUNCIL

HOLLY AND I enjoy an easy morning; the kind long-time married couples have. Despite the short time we've been together, we're like a comfortable pair of old slippers. Small talk at breakfast, a leisurely walk on the beach, and a nap in the late morning.

Since my Parkinson's symptoms disappeared, I've forgotten I had it. Another thing I notice is I haven't uttered the word *cellphone* since I arrived. Ask me if I miss it? You gotta be kidding. I'm in paradise with a woman I adore, a place where everything I need or want magically appears. Whatcha think?

I peer out at the ocean. "I wonder if I should join some avian friends and head out for a lazy afternoon."

Holly looks over her sunglasses. "That's not on your agenda today."

"I have an agenda today? This is the first I've heard about it."

"Yeah, you need to attend a council meeting."

"Council meeting?"

"You didn't think we can skip a day of training, did you? You're not going to stay here forever."

I head to the kitchen and grab a cold one. Returning, I sit so we face each other. "For a minute there, I thought you said I had to attend some sort of meeting."

"That's the deal. And...you have to go by yourself while I stay behind."

I've never seen her face so expressionless.

"Are you serious?"

"Yes, I am. Let me tell you the plan."

"Go ahead. I'm listening."

"You remember several days ago when we took the hike inland. You are to follow that same path and whenever you come to a fork in the road, take it." She giggles with delight. "At least that's what Yogi Berra would say."

Upon hearing a favorite Yogi Berra quote, I breathe a sigh of relief and take another drink of beer.

Holly winks. "Okay, just follow the road *more traveled*—not the one less traveled. That is, if you prefer a Robert Frost quote more than the one from Yogi."

I love it when she gets squirrely.

"You can go dressed as you are, but you need to wear a special timepiece. When you've walked for eighty-five minutes *exactly,* sit down on the nearest log and sing the *Happy Wanderer* song using your best baritone voice. But only sing the first verse. Then sit still, be patient, and wait. Soon your guide will appear and take you to the meeting."

I look for a wristwatch. Yup, there's one on my left wrist. Nothing special about it; probably cost ten bucks at Walmart. Actually looks more like a Fitbit; a lot more than ten bucks.

"May I ask what sort of people make up *this council?*"

"Of course. They are your colleagues. They're mostly famous physicians from history."

"Really?"

Holly chuckles, "You'll figure it out when you get there. But get going now. Your eighty-five minutes just started."

"How fast should I walk?"

"Makes no difference, Doctor Andresen. Just get going."

I walk over the rise behind the cabin. The view is different from the last time; more forests, fewer ponds, no flowing creeks. How the heck am I supposed to choose the road more traveled? What I can't figure out is why my speed doesn't matter. There's a big difference in how far you go if you're walking three miles an hour versus five. I take my time to pull a small strip of bark from a beechnut tree and taste the cambium layer. It's a main source of food for beavers. A lot of people don't know cambium can be food for humans too. Since speed makes no difference, I amuse myself nosing into whatever else I choose.

I stop when my Fitbit buzzes. I should've known Holly would make sure I stop at the right time; eighty-five minutes exactly, to the second.

I look for a downed tree to sit on and find one ten yards from the path. Looks like a blue spruce that's been here awhile, its trunk is bare. If I'm going to sound like a booming baritone, I better remain standing with my arms at my sides. I warm up singing some *do-re-mes,* loosen my abdominal muscles, and tilt my head to the sky.

*"I love to go a-wandering..."*

I'm surprised at the richness of my voice. Parkinson's often muffles the voice and really messes up singing. Just ask Linda Ronstadt. While I'm no Pavarotti; today I think I could audition for the Norman Luboff Choir.

Finished with my song, I sit and wait, wondering who my guide will be. Soon I catch sight of something running through the forest. Looks like it might be a small dog, but as it approaches, its red coat and white-tipped tail make clear it's a fox. It sits in front of me making steady eye contact. Domestic dogs thrive looking at human faces. Wolves, coyotes and foxes never look at humans directly. This fox is an exception; it's looking me in the eye and smiling. I think she's female; just something about the look in her eyes. She shakes her head vigorously causing her collar to jingle. I reach down to examine it. Attached is a small bell and a tag with writing on it. *Babette, fox guide.* I wonder why it says, 'fox guide' instead of 'guide fox.'

Babette sits on her haunches and offers me a paw. "Dr. Peter Andresen, I presume."

"Yes, that's me."

"A *guide dog* is a service animal for people with disabilities. A *dog guide* is precisely that. You're not disabled, but you don't know where to go. Hence, I've been assigned to guide you to the Council meeting."

"Talking with you, Babette, reminds me of Dr. Doolittle. He was a medical doctor who quit treating humans and chose instead to treat animals. He was special, he could talk with all animals. I feel like a modern Dr. Doolittle."

Babette stops to scratch her collar. Finished she sits before me, "You're not Dr. Doolittle."

"What makes you so sure?"

"Dr. Doolittle is the Chairman of the Council. You'll meet him shortly. Shall we get going?"

At a loss for words, I mumble, "Okay...I guess."

A thin overcast and cheerful breezes cool us on our way.

Like Barney, Babette runs ahead, stops, and waits for me to catch up. As I catch up, she runs further ahead. We repeat this pattern several times.

*I might be lost but I'm making good time.*

When I stop for a breather, I hear people talking in the distance, talking. I can't make out what they're saying, but I think the voices are male. Babette reappears and sits in front of me.

"Dr. Andresen, pay attention. Here's what's going to happen. We'll walk side by side into the meeting. I will take you to Dr. Doolittle who will introduce you. The purpose of the council is to clarify your thinking about medicine, the mind, and what you'll do when you return to material reality."

Wow. I'm about to be in the company of the greatest medical minds in history. I hope I don't screw up. And...I hope they have a good sense of humor

Babette sneezes. "Sense of humor? You're headed to the right place."

"Why do you say that?"

"These guys—and they're all guys—know the importance of a merry heart. Shall we move on?"

"Why is it just guys?"

"They used to make all the rules."

Heeling at my left, she marches with a stately, deliberate stride. Soon, we enter a well-mowed green meadow surrounded by forest. A brook murmurs along the far side. Several men sit on high-backed chairs arranged in an oval. Each chair has a nameplate affixed to the back. I recognize several names right away: Sir William Osler, Hippocrates of Kos, Galen, Vesalius. At the left of each chair, a small table is covered with a variety of beverages, finger foods, and bowls of fruit.

Babette marches to the one man standing—I presume he is Dr. Doolittle. She sits waiting to be acknowledged.

Dr. Doolittle isn't what I expected. He wears a black waistcoat with a starched white shirt and a red plaid double-breasted vest and on his head, a black stovepipe hat. But instead of looking like some standard white guy, he looks exactly like Eddie Murphy.

He winks at Babette. She answers, "Here's Dr. Peter Andresen."

When bidden, Babette jumps into Dr. Doolittle's arms, while at the same time, the good doctor offers me his hand. "Welcome, Dr. Andresen. It is a pleasure to have you as our guest. First thing you need to know is, this gathering is very informal. We've chosen to go by handles. None of us is addressed as doctor. I'm called, Doodle. What would you like us to call you?"

Not feeling creative, I say, "You can call me, Peter."

Doodle fakes a grimace. "That's pedestrian. How about Andy? Short for Andresen."

"Well, that's what my father was called when he was in school. Works for me."

"Come, sit next to me."

The chair is like all the others, straight with a tall back bearing a bronze nameplate. Mine reads. *Peter Andresen, Shrink..*

Doodle chuckles. "Andy, we like handles—at least we call them handles— when speaking with each other. They're intended for kidding or good-natured teasing. We're all about having fun while still addressing the big stuff.

Babette jumps down and takes her place on a doggie bed

beside Doodle. I look around the group. Each man wears different clothes, representing different times and cultures. Next to me, a bearded guy is wearing a toga and leather sandals. His plaque reads, *Hippocrates of Kos, Father of Medicine.*

"Okay, everyone, listen up. This is Dr. Peter Andresen. I've been told he has a pretty good sense of humor."

I nod at the circle of smiling faces

"Andy, as he's asked to be called, is here to gather our shared lofty wisdom relating to the Body-Mind. He will return to material reality soon and is certain to benefit from whatever you want to share. As always, we won't follow *Robert's Rules of Order*. We haven't been dead this long just to have to follow some freaking rules. And remember our one rule relating to humor. Use liberally."

The council applauds politely and says in unison, "Hi, Andy." Their greeting reminds me of an AA meeting.

Hippocrates speaks first. "My name is Hippa, I'm the father of medicine."

His introduction spurs a number of catcalls. He responds with a dismissive finger gesture and directs his words to me. "How much do you know about me?"

"When I think about it, I know very little. I took The Hippocratic Oath when I became a doctor. I think you lived around four hundred B.C.E."

"Yeah, that's about all most people know. The first biography about me was written six hundred years after I died. Needless to say, I'm mostly mythical. But several critical medical practices were attributed to me—some true and still relevant. Others, like bloodletting took too long to die. Remember when you documented the so-called exorcisms? You kept accurate records."

"You know that about me?"

A man seated next to Hippa signals he would like to speak.

His nameplate reads, *Sir William Osler, Father of Modern Medicine.* I recognize Dr. Osler. His picture graces the walls of many medical schools. But, if I had to list what I know about him;

it would be a short list. He appears to be comfortable wearing a three-piece tweed suit and a black bow tie.

"Andy, we have information all about your life and thought. Assume we know everything about you. Your mind is an open book."

"Dr. Osler, what am I supposed to call you?"

Several men chuckle. Sir William answers, "At first I asked to be called, Willy, but Willy Shakespeare had claimed that handle already. So, we settled on calling me Ozzie."

I feel more at ease. "Okay, Ozzie. I'm all ears."

"While Hippa and I are separated by twenty-three centuries, we share a quote attributed to both of us. '*It is much more important to know what patient has the disease than what disease the patient has.*' The power of a patient's mind is rarely considered in current allopathic medicine practice."

Hippa adds, I'm best known for declaring medicine to be independent of religion. Illness had been thought to be a punishment by whatever god was popular at the time. I posited illness had a physical and rational explanation. That conclusion was based on my medical practice and observations. I studied the body, but it would be six hundred years before my noble friend and colleague, Galen of Pergamon, dissected a body to learn anatomy."

A voice across the oval shouts, "Dammit, Hippa, my handle is Galenco. Use my handle or I'll call you Ozzie and Harriet."

Hippa looks startled. "No offense intended."

"Intended or not, it ticks me off."

Doodle whispers in my ear. "Those two have been going at it for nearly two millennia. I think Galenco is still offended by Hippa's fame. Galenco kept Hippa's work in the mainstream. Who knows where medical history would be if Galenco hadn't written so lavishly about Hippa's work?"

Galenco and Hippa continue to argue. Hippa tries to calm the waters. "You were a great physician. It's just that you came after me. It was if you were in my shadow. And let me remind you, it would be over a thousand years before human beings were actually dissected. You substituted a pig's anatomy for human's."

"Don't remind me. You know it was against the law to dissect humans. A guy could be executed if he dissected a human body. I know de Luzzi, performed the first legal human dissection to study anatomy. Happened in Bologna I believe."

Galenco stops and looks around. Anybody know if Luci was going to be here?"

Doodle stands and waits for the chatter to diminish. "Do I need to remind you we're here to assist Andy? Let's limit discussion to what his needs will be when he returns. And no, Galenco, Luci won't be here."

Ozzie picks up where he left off. "Andy, do you see how long it's taken medicine to evolve? Imagine, it took seventeen hundred years to simply arrive at Anatomy 101."

"I've never looked at it that way."

"You remember Scrooge from *A Christmas Carol*? Do you recall the two urchins under the skirt of *Christmas Present*. They were named *Ignorance* and *Want*. Which one is to be more feared?"

"Ignorance."

"Absolutely. Medicine has been in mortal conflict with Ignorance from the beginning of time. Still is. Look at your enlightened twenty-first century. Diphtheria and tetanus are virtually non-existent. Why? Immunizations. Eddie Jenner must be turning over in his grave seeing how ignorance is motivating people to avoid immunizations."

Ozzie slaps his hand over his mouth. "The very thought I would use Eddie Jenner and a cliché in the same sentence...Sorry, Eddie."

Across the oval, a jolly voice answers. "No offense taken, Ozzie. To tell the truth, if I were in a grave now, I certainly would roll over—or better yet, rise from the dead and get back to work."

Shaking his head, Ozzie continues. "The greater the ignorance, the greater the dogmatism. And that brings to mind that I must caution you: Be careful talking to people about your understanding of the infinite mind. If, by some alignment of the stars, your thought becomes popular, you know it will be distorted. It will be seen as both heresy and gospel."

"I doubt my thinking will affect anybody except the few I'm able to help."

"Probably so, but the future is still unknown."

"That surprises me, Ozzie. I thought you and my guides, like Holly and Solomon would know the future."

Ozzie smiles like a first-grade teacher peering into a student's brain. "I doubt any of your guides foresee the future. None of us can. It is one of the firm boundaries. We might have a pretty good idea of what will happen, but none of us knows."

"What about the laws of physics?"

"Do you remember Nicolaus Copernicus?"

"Yeah, he was the first to say the sun was the center of the universe."

Ozzie turns to Doodle. "I don't see Nickie? Why isn't he here today."

"He wanted to be part of the astrophysics council."

"Andy, what else do you know about Nickie C?"

"Not much,"

"He was one hell of a physician and an engineer too. There was a great epidemic in 1519 in Poland. Understanding clean water could stop the epidemic, he engineered a water supply for two towns that stopped them."

"Did he know about germs?"

"I don't know. We'll ask next time we run into him."

My head goes tilt like a jolted pinball machine.

Doodle addresses the gathering. "We will reconvene tomorrow and continue Andy's training. Before we part I would like the Jungature to tell us one of his famous jokes. We all know he spent years studying the difference between female and male minds."

"The Jungature?"

"Yeah, that's the handle Carl Jung chose. Many of these

learned men have great senses of humor. Ozzie loves practical jokes. The Jungature loves jokes about the sexes."

The famous psychiatrist wears a tweed suit and a white shirt with an open collar. He bows deeply and starts his routine.

"There are five ways for a man to be completely happy .First, be with a woman who makes you laugh. Second, be with a woman who gives you her time. Third, a woman to take care of you. Fourth, a with a woman who really loves you. And finally, make sure these four women don't know each other."

The men of this distinguished gathering break into side-splitting laughter. I thought it was pretty funny, too. A bit sexist, but I think back to the time most of these men lived. Women were excluded because men thought them inferior in almost every way.

The group disperses and the men wander off, merging into the surrounding forest. That leaves Doodle, Babette, and me the last to leave.

"Doodle, what am I supposed to do now?"

"Babette will guide you to shelter where you will spend the night. You might be alone or you might not. You might meet very famous teachers. And about the next council, I'm going to delay it awhile. You're going to have a lot on your plate."

I feel Babette's teeth close gently on my hand. Then she walks me back the way we came. Soon, we too disappear into the forest.

# CHAPTER 12
# JESSE

DARKNESS FALLS AS if hurrying to get on with other matters. Following Babette, I see why she was equipped with a white tip on her tail. We follow a twisting path, climbing steeper the further we go. I'm completely out of breath when we arrive at the top. There, I enter an orchard containing countless varieties of fruit trees.

Some distance away, I hear Babette bark, which is most unusual. Thus far, I've only heard her speak English with a Canadian accent. Her tail switches back and forth, helping me to locate her. She stands near a circle of tall stones that remind me of Stonehenge, only on a smaller scale.

Upon entering, a crackling campfire welcomes me. An ample stack of firewood near the fire assures me I'll have sufficient light and warmth until morning. Babette scurries around as if she's making sure everything's in order. When finished, she sits in front of me offering her paw.

"What's the plan, Babette? What's in store for me tonight?"

She tilts her head to the side as if trying to understand what I said. Not speaking a word, she dances around and playfully jumps on me. After a dozen jumps, she stops and extends her front legs while holding her rump in the air. Jumping to her feet, she barks twice and then sprints into the forest.

I look out from my mini-Stonehenge and become transfixed by a spectacular full moon. I think it's the first time I've seen the moon in imaginary reality. But it's not the moon I'm familiar with. It's smoother, almost like a giant cue ball.

I didn't eat much at the council, so now I'm seriously hungry. I nose around; there's gotta be food here. In a second, I discover a reusable plastic grocery bag filled with picnic essentials: Hebrew National wieners, hot dog buns, Lays classic potato chips, Coca-Cola, graham crackers, squares of Dove dark chocolate, and mini marshmallows. A veritable feast. Long sticks for cooking wieners and roasting marshmallows lie on the ground near the food. I sit on a flat rock to enjoy my boy scout picnic. First the hot dogs, second the smores, and I finish by drinking two cokes. I return the scraps to the plastic bag wondering if they recycle here. Finished with supper, I walk out to gaze at the moon again. The breeze rustling the trees is the only sound. I'm indeed alone. I half expected Holly to be here, but she's not. So, I embark on a listening walk alone.

I recall the difference between being lonely and being alone. Loneliness has plagued me since Annie died. Tonight, I'm alone, but not lonely. Then again, it would be nice to talk with another great wisdom figure; one who knows the power of mind and how it heals.

Upon returning to mini Stonehenge, I discover a bed has been prepared. It consists of two wool blankets covering a thick mattress of straw. On one end there's a bundled sheepskin; it must be my pillow. The fire is burning down, making this the best time to study the glowing embers. For millennia, humankind has experienced comfort while gazing at a dwindling fire...and slowly drifting into slumber just as I am now.

For my first fifty years, I always ended my day with standard Christian prayers. But, not anymore. I'm not going to think about it tonight. No more theological contemplation. As I lie down, I imagine the infinite mind flowing around and through my being. I'm careful to harbor no expectations.

Sometime later, a disturbing dream interrupts my sleep. A mob of angry people chant and mill around; many shake their fists over their heads. I cannot understand the language. But the feelings are jarring and feel like shredding glass, filled with hate and anger. I want no part of this. A horde of poisoned minds. What am I doing here? I want out, but the crowd tightens until I cannot move. There is no escape.

Something benevolent intervenes forcing me to wake with a start. As my mind settles, I ease back onto my mattress.

Something's changed. I'm aware I'm not alone. I sit up and watch as a man adds wood to the fire. He's about five foot five and his skin is a dark shade of middle-eastern. His wide nose and full lips suggest African ancestry. Loose, curly black hair frames his face which is covered by a full beard. His modest dress consists of a tunic with a belt. I'm affected by his presence. I feel soothing peacefulness flowing through my body. Simply observing him, imbues me with a deep calm. He's like an old friend I fail to recognize. Turning his attention to me, the warmth of his smile radiates from his widely-spaced, stained teeth and generous lips.

For several minutes we simply look at one another. It's an odd silence, but not uncomfortable. Finally, I get up and walk outside to relieve myself. Upon my I return; I find my companion seated on a three-legged stool. He motions for me to sit on another stool next to him. We fixate on the magic of the fire until he breaks the silence.

"Hello, Peter. I'm sure you're wondering who I am, so let me tell you a few things about myself. By reputation, I am considered by some to be the most important healer in history. But, let's be clear, we always need to be skeptical about reputations. They are a collection of thoughts held by a close-knit group of people who share a common agenda. They will shape their chosen healer to fit their beliefs. I'm sure you recall the myth of Procrustes and his one-size-fits-all bed. A group of people creating a reputation for their chosen one do a similar thing. If their chosen person is too tall, they cut their legs off so they fit the Procrustean bed. If they're too short, stretch them on a rack until they fit."

"What is your name?"

"While I was alive, I was called, *Yeshua*. To this day, people continue to call me that. But for you and me, here tonight, I prefer you call me Jesse"

I'm surprised, but I'm not speechless and overwhelmed by what he's saying. I simply respond, "Yeshua is Aramaic for Jesus."

Jesse takes a thick stick and prods the fire. "That it is."

My next response is banal. "You don't look like Jesus."

Jesse laughs so hard he falls backward on the ground, shaking his frame as he rolls from side to side. When he stops laughing, he regains his composure and sits back on his stool.

"Don't you love it, Peter? Almost everyone alive has an image of me being a tall white guy, with flowing light brown hair and blue eyes. But look at me...here...today. This is exactly how I looked when I lived on earth. I'm a lot more African than Caucasian. It's in my DNA. And no, my DNA has no 'God-The-Father' genes."

My next comment is playful sarcasm. "Won't the Ku Klux Klan be pissed when they find that out?"

Jesse chuckles. "I thought you and I would hit it off."

I add, "It's not only the Klan that is clueless. My wife and I were granted permission to go inside a newly built Mormon Temple before it was consecrated. I thought it was beautiful, but non-historical and blatantly racist. Paintings throughout the Temple depict you as you described; a tall white guy dressed in white flowing clothes with red or purple cloaks, a perfect smile and deep blue eyes."

"Peter, you have no idea what it's been like for me to witness how, not just my appearance, but the heart of my teachings have been distorted by my so-called followers."

"I never thought there was a link between your teachings and waging war. But I went to war and I did kill people by dropping bombs on them."

"You still feel guilty about that...right?"

"Yeah. After the war, I became a member of the Society of Friends—a Quaker. And at the same time, despite having killed people, I was proud to have been a Marine."

"Becoming a Marine was your effort to feel accepted and be counted on as a person who will do anything to save a friend. How did you feel when you dropped the bombs?"

"I didn't feel much of anything. I felt I was just doing my job by the book. I never visualized what happened when my bombs hit their target."

"That's what happens in the mind of a warrior: denial and repression. But don't come to me seeking forgiveness. That's not in my job description. As a healer, you must forgive yourself first. More about that another day."

I'm unsure what to do or say next. Jesse breaks the silence. "I feel like a drink. How about you?"

"Oh yes, Jess. Great idea. Just what I need, too."

"Your choice," Jesse says. "Holly left me this box. Whatever we want to drink will be in the box when you open it. Go ahead. Introduce me to something new."

I open the box and behold an old favorite, *Highland Park* Scotch, twenty-five years old.

"Jesse, you know much about scotch?"

"Can't say I do. Tell me what I need to know. While I was alive, we only drank wine—not very good stuff, but it did the job. The alcohol killed bacteria."

"Did you really pull off that water into wine gig?"

"Nope. My followers thought it would serve to get me good press and get off the *sin-talk* for a while."

"Okay, Jess, here's what you do: single malt scotch has varying amounts of alcohol when it's bottled. So, you pour your dram into a glass. Then you add water, a teaspoon at a time, until it's just right for you."

We mix our whiskey libation with some pomp and circumstance and then settle back to enjoy it, one sip at a time. We talk about superficial things like baseball and my love of Yogi Berra quotes. When we finish, Jesse returns to our earlier discussion.

"When people came to be healed and got better, I refused to take credit for the healing. I said things like 'Your faith has made you whole.' Or, 'Go to the Temple and show your body to the Priests and do as they say.'"

"What did you mean by the word, *faith*?"

"It is a deeply-held mindset you develop that says, *Yes, I can*. Of course, you can be modern and look up faith on Wikipedia: *Now faith is the substance of things hoped for, the evidence of things not seen*. Or, *Faith is the connecting power into the spiritual realm, which links us with God and makes Him become a tangible reality to the sense perceptions of a person*."

"The latter makes more sense to me"

"Well, it's closer, but it still maintains God is an entity and also masculine. A rabbi friend once said, 'The true God has as much gender as a table.'"

I bust a gut laughing. "Great line."

"And, Peter, don't confuse a healer with a miracle worker. While you're at it, don't think a healer has to be a saint. Sainthood is another concept created by human minds. It doesn't have any God juice."

I chuckle. "God juice?"

"Yeah, or you could call it God mojo, if you prefer."

"Jesse, why did we meet like this? Why not at a Council? I mean, our meeting appears to be a case of special handling."

"It is designed to have maximum effect on your unconscious mind. Remember, when you return to your life, you will not remember these experiences. But...they will have a profound effect on your mind. Few people are provided this opportunity. You will behave differently and affect people as you never have before. But—and this is a big but—you will not feel special. You will not stand out. You will simply be a part of infinite mind evolving throughout the Universe."

Bewildered, I lean back and study the fire. "Jesse, I can't wrap my head around there being no God."

Jesse takes a minute before responding. "The infinite mind, the Author—if you will—of the Big Bang cannot be compre-hended by the human mind. Every time someone tries to, they diminish that reality. But perhaps you're at the point where you can use the word, *God*, without diminishing the reality of its infinity."

"I started this whole affair while walking alone on a beach. I met Holly and felt it was going to be a lot of fun and games. And now, I'm here talking with the historical Jesus. And I'm being indoctrinated—shaped—to become a healer; a concept I don't really understand. I haven't a clue how this fits into the *big picture*—or if there is any so-called *big picture* at all. How am I supposed to feel? At the moment, I'm just feeling confused and irritated."

"It's not unusual for people like you to express any number of questions or irritations. It's a sign of how safe they feel. When you grew up as a Christian, you would never say you're irritated with Jesus. And here you just did."

"You're right. My mind is a mix of competing thoughts. On the other hand, when I look inside, I feel honored, special."

"And so you are."

"How did it happen that you became the greatest healer in history?"

"Funny, it started out following much the same path you are on now."

I gulp. "Jesse, I need to get on my feet and walk around a bit."

"I understand. Your mind is synced with the infinite mind. Though you aren't aware of it, the mind is downloading its essence as we speak."

"That may be. But the only thing I'm aware of at the moment is needing to take a leak."

Jesse laughs. "How perfectly human of you."

Walking outside, I look at the sky. The moon is setting while on the opposite horizon I see the first sunbeams of morning. I whisper, "This is the day the Lord has made. I will rejoice and be glad in it."

I take care of my business and return to find Jesse has a visitor whose clothing leaves no doubt about his identity. Feeling more confident and brash, I approach the saffron-robed visitor and extend my hand, "Gautama Buddha, I presume."

He responds with a Dalai Lama smile. "Hello, Peter, welcome to our sangha. But, please, I prefer you call me Siddhartha, or Sid for short."

I respond, "The last Syd I met was a rabbi, but I suspect you spell your name with an 'I' not a 'Y.'"

Jesse and Sid nod. "The rebbi is one of us, too."

"How many people like you are there?"

Sid answers. "In Buddhism, we have a name for healers, they're called bodhisattvas. They have achieved Buddhahood, but are driven by compassion to repeatedly return to life until every human becomes a Buddha. They don't rest on their laurels."

Jesse adds, "My followers find it more difficult. Many believe so strongly in sin, that even very devoted people spend their lives languishing in guilt. I appreciate a recent response for Christian guilt-mongers, *I don't need to be born again, I was born right the first time*."

Sid smiles broadly. "We're getting tangled in Earth thinking. Healers come from everywhere, every religion or no religion at all. Hippa was the first to separate medicine from religion. What you need to learn, Peter, are the characteristics of healers—not where they come from."

Jesse nods. "The principal reason you're here now is because you've practiced empathy and understanding from the earliest days of your life. Now you have arrived at the place where you let go of all man-made ideas about God. You believe in reason. And you practice kindness."

My vision starts changing, blurring, shimmering. My hearing becomes muted like I'm at the end of a long tunnel. Jesse and Sid fade. I'm suspended in space. Three words reverberate in my mind:

*Empathy*

*Kindness*
*Understanding*

I recite them over and over. They grow into a chant filling my entire being. Multi-colored clouds float around me. I wonder, *Is this the infinite mind?*

Two words resound in my mind: "I AM."

# CHAPTER 13
# UNDERSTANDING

S TANDING BESIDE A five foot kumquat tree, I pick one yellow fruit no larger than a grape.

*What does a guy do after spending a night with Jesus?*

I don't have an answer, but I feel I should immerse my mind in simplicity and play. It's all about balance. I decide to summon an old childhood chum, Bugs Bunny. I came to know Bugs and his antagonist, Marvin the Martian, while in elementary school and during those college afternoons when I watched Gidget movies. There is something pure about Looney Tunes characters. Their anger is never real. Nobody really gets hurt. Anxiety is non-existent. Wile E. Coyote can go kaboom a thousand times and always come back to chase the roadrunner again. That's the mindset I'm looking for this morning.

Overhead, scattered clouds linger. They're ideal for projecting images of my mind. I lie on the ground and sort through cartoon reruns, limiting my selection to Bugs and Marvin. I pick a large flat-bottomed cloud to be my screen. I choose my favorite episode where Marvin tries to destroy the Earth (again) with his *Illudium Q-36 Explosive Space Modulator*. His motivation? The Earth blocks his view of Venus. When Bugs gets wind of Marvin's plans, he spends the next ten minutes maneuvering around Marvin. Not only does the Earth survive, Marvin's the one who goes kaboom. Love it!

Cartoon over, but I'm still out of sorts. Who you gonna call? Holly, of course. I envision her arriving on the back of my owl taxi. Knowing she'll arrive when the time is right, I return to mini-Stonehenge only to discover she's there and has breakfast ready.

"I understand you met a couple guys who loom large in world history last night. Is that why you asked me to come?"

"It is. I feel like a nearly completed jigsaw puzzle with several missing pieces."

Holly stops what she's doing. "Here, Peter, come with me." She takes my hand, "Forget about breakfast. I'm taking you somewhere more suitable for talking; a place to fit your pieces together." She snaps her fingers and a second later, I'm full, like I just consumed a sumptuous breakfast.

We leave the rock circle and find our owl taxi ready to go. Crawling onto its back is still a strange experience to say the least. But in Holly's world, everything is strange.

"Close your eyes, Peter, and keep holding my hand. I have the perfect place where we can go talk."

Doing as Holly instructed, I nestle into owl feathers and fall asleep. When I wake, Holly and I are floating in a gorgeous hot spring nestled in an immense green valley surrounded by towering mountains. The water is so buoyant, it could have come from the dead sea. Everything else in this place feels totally alive...*perfect*. I wonder where we are. The surrounding mountains remind me of the Himalayas.

"Yes, those are the Himalayas," Holly says. "This specific place is named *Shangri La*, a mythical happy land, isolated from the world."

"Shangri La...paradise...heaven. I'd like to grow old here. Can you arrange that?"

Holly winks. "Sorry, that's above my pay grade."

I spent last night engaging with the two most influential luminaries in history. I mean...I was in awe when I was young and shook hands with John Kennedy, but drinking Scotch with Jesus and Siddhartha Buddha and talking about the meaning of life...by a campfire...?

Nothing else comes to mind, so I turn my attention to the

sky and ease into an unprepared monologue. "I remember Joseph Campbell's description of *The Hero's Journey*. An everyday guy finds himself inexplicably in a region of supernatural wonder. He encounters an adversary or situation which puts him at great risk. He meets that test and overcomes it. As a result, he gains wisdom or supernatural powers which he brings back to benefit humankind.

"Am I on a hero's journey? It seems like it. But what's my challenge? Who will be my adversary? What can be greater than talking with Jesus and The Buddha? Or is it like the old Peggy Lee tune, *Is that all there is?*"

My thinking stops, like the end of a vinyl record; just click, click, click until you lift the needle.

Holly appears more thoughtful than usual. "Let's take some time for you to tell me what's going on in your mind. I know what it is, but you need to talk about it using your own words."

Although there are no chairs, we sit suspended in water up to our chins. Holly's wearing a hibiscus in her hair and a yellow polka-dot bikini. I look down and discover I'm wearing an old fashioned two-piece swimsuit. It's right out of the Twenties, just like the one *The Great Gatsby* wore; a black and white striped top, a black canvas belt, and white swimming trunks.

"You mentioned *The Hero's Journey* and wonder where you fit. I want you to understand this: you passed your undergraduate tests before you arrived. That's why you're here. Look at the trials and tragedies you've lived through. All your life, you've been tested. Let me illustrate by asking you one simple question: How do you feel about your mother? Now...here...today."

Not prepared for serious talk, I quip, "A Freudian slip is when you say one thing, but mean your mother."

Holly dunks me. "Really, Peter, I expected something more original from you."

I blow a tablespoon of saltwater from my nose. "Once you start making Freudian slips, it's just one after your mother."

This time Holly dunks her own head. When she comes up,

she's loosened her ponytail and pulled her auburn hair over her face.

"The creature from the black lagoon, I presume?"

She dunks me again and this time holds me under until I realize I'm in imaginary reality and I can breathe under water.

Back to sitting in nonexistent chairs and floating in dead sea water, Holly impersonates a scolding first grade teacher. "Peter, let's get serious or I'll have to send you home." Her playful tone fails to conceal something deeper on her mind.

"Okay, I'll get serious, but first how about you conjure a pitcher of Mai Tais?"

Leaving the pool, we wrap ourselves in white terrycloth robes and sit by a small table with a pitcher of Mai Tais and a basket of fruit. I spot some kumquats that must have come along on our owl ride.

Now looking like a nurse about to give me a shot, Holly folds her arms. "I love your playful sense of humor, but sometimes, humor is used to avoid an uncomfortable subject."

I get the message and settle down. A long pause follows until I realize I'm on center-stage and it's time for another monologue.

"Mom didn't have an easy life. My sibs, Kate and Terry, never forgave her, carrying their bitter feelings to the end of their lives. During my high school years, Mom and I spent many evenings together, mostly watching TV. Because, after school, I always went to the library and did my homework which meant once I was home, there wasn't much to do. So, there were evenings she told me about her early life. It wasn't pretty.

"Her father was Danish and emigrated to Iowa in the late nineteenth century. He homesteaded there and started a family. Fifteen years later, there was a tragic house fire. His wife tried to save the children, throwing them from upstairs windows to my grandfather below. Before she finished, the floor gave way. She and the two youngest children perished.

"My grandfather couldn't farm and take care of five children by himself, so he paid the ocean fare and imported a woman from Norway to do the job. It was a business arrangement until she became pregnant a few years later. My mother didn't know that history until decades later. She was born the day after their minister forced my Grandfather to marry my Grandmother or risk excommunication. Fleeing shame, my grandfather moved to North Dakota to start over. Once there, Mom's two half-sisters moved away to live with another family. They even took the family's last name. Mom grew up hardly knowing them.

"Her three older brothers who stayed with my grandfather died early, tragic deaths. One drowned in a hunting accident. One died in World War I. The last was murdered. That left Mom and her parents alone on a desolate quarter-section of land ten miles from the nearest town. When Mom was ten, her father had a stroke and died. That meant Mom and her mother were alone and penniless. All they owned were their clothes and a few sticks of furniture. The farm went bankrupt forcing them to move into town."

My mouth dry from talking, I pour another Mai Tai and grab a handful of kumquats before I continue.

"Allow me a slight diversion; a little-known piece of history comes into play. As an ethnic group, Scandinavians in America were thought to be homogeneous. Their traits were described several ways, including hard-working, taciturn, God-fearing, and dull. What isn't widely known are the deep divisions among Norwegians, Danes, and Swedes just after they arrived from Europe.

"The history of Denmark and Norway is particularly contentious going back to the twelfth century. Norway was not a feudal society. Young men were required to perform all the farm labor and delay marriage until their thirties or even their forties. And today most people think Garrison Keillor made up the concept of *Norwegian Bachelor Farmers*. But they've been around for over eight centuries."

Holly stops me. "Wait a minute. I thought you were telling me about your mother's difficult life."

"I am. Trust me, this will make sense in a minute."

Holly lifts an eyebrow and finishes her Mai Tai.

I resume. "The Black death killed nearly two-thirds of Norway's population in 1349. It was worst along the coast where ships brought more bubonic plague every time one managed to dock. One result was the Norwegians living on the coast who were the most educated were also most likely to die. Farmers working farther away from the coast had a lower mortality. The Danes came to rescue Norway by bringing educated businesspeople and the clergy. Quickly, a two-class system evolved; uneducated hardworking Norwegian farmers and scholarly, pious Danes.

"That separation continued to the 1880s when Scandinavians settled in Wisconsin, Minnesota, and the Dakotas. How this affected my mother was no laughing matter. She was a half Norwegian girl being raised in a one hundred percent Danish community. Kids called her 'half-breed' describing her to be dumber than a fence post. She was ostracized and the victim of disdainful teasing.

"She and her mother moved into a small room above a candy store. Their sole income came from her mother taking in laundry. Mom did not do well in school because she didn't understand math, so the school arranged for her to graduate by taking extra home-economics classes.

"I don't know what she did during the years following high school. But somehow, five years later, she made it into nurses' training in Minot and became an RN. Very smart move; an excellent achievement. She met and married my father after she graduated. The Great Depression was in full swing so they delayed having children.

"Dad welcomed my Grandmother; in part, because they were both pure Norwegian. She lived with them the last seven years of her life. But when Grandma died, Mom's two Danish half-sisters swooped in and told Mom she was a bastard and they had the signed Bible to prove it. After that, Mom descended into a black hole depression from which she never completely emerged."

I stop. My lip quivering; I feel very sad.

"Your mother's life was a great deal more difficult than yours," Holly says. "She never overcame her chronic anger and depression."

"No, she didn't. But she did work as a nurse off and on for several years. My parent's didn't have much money, but together they prided themselves for never having *gone on relief.*"

Holly takes my sweaty hand. "What do you feel about your mother here, today?"

"It's funny in a way. Ever since Mom died, I'm remembering more of our happy times—and there were some. I remember her baking cookies and pies, and her being so proud I became a doctor. When we watched TV together, we laughed a lot."

I pause, remembering Holly's questions—how do I *feel* about Mom now?

"I never did like her very much. I don't recall ever loving her. But then again, I never hated her either. Here and now? That doesn't make any difference. More than anything, I *understand* how she became the way she was. I also know, intimately, what untreated depression does to the brain—how extremely difficult her life was. I'm so glad when the first antidepressant was approved, she took it and it helped."

Holly smiles. "See what you've done? Long before you had your family, you practiced empathy, compassion and understanding. Look how long it took to summarize your mom's life just now. Understanding takes time, commitment, and work. Above all, it can only start when you cease being judgmental."

No longer ready to tell another joke, I hang my head and I sob. I cry for Mom and I cry that I never had *a real mom.* Gradually I regain awareness of my surroundings. I love it here. And I know it's a mythical place. Once I leave, I'll not return.

Holly senses I've competed my work. "Before we depart, Peter, is there something you'd like?"

"Yeah, a chocolate malted milkshake with a cherry on top."

No sooner do I ask, than we're sitting at a soda fountain. The malted milkshake is served in a large glass and with more remaining in the metal mixing canister. "I haven't enjoyed one of these since the sixties."

Finished, we call our owl taxi. When we climb on, I fall asleep.

# CHAPTER 14
# BE

O UR MORNING IS one of peace and positivity. We sit on the porch watching birds, dolphins, clouds, and each other. Our chairs are close enough that we take the other's hand to hold it next to our cheek. We kiss each other on the lips less frequently than when we first met. The love we share is rich, but requires less passion to express it.

I've lost track of how long I've been here. I know I must return to my material reality, but my wish is to stay here forever. For me, this *is* heaven. I have no symptoms of Parkinson's. My past no longer troubles me. I can look back on my life and see mistakes—a lot of them. But acceptance has replaced remorse. My past is what it is and nothing more. Old painful feelings are like an ashtray filled with cigarette butts. Both should be discarded.

Holly stands and stretches. "Let me take you to some different places today, each spectacular in its own way."

"So long as there are no airplanes involved."

"Silly man, you know how unappealing material reality can be. Life in imaginary reality is only limited by our mind."

"You haven't called me silly man for a while. Once I got used to it, I liked it. It became a term of endearment."

Holly skootches close. "What do you know about starlings?"

"A little. I think they're an invasive species that came from Europe. In big flocks, they pose a threat to airplanes by getting sucked into jet engines. Tell the truth, they're not my favorite bird."

Holly frowns. "Aren't you the ornithologist? Do you have any other unfavorable opinions about them?"

Feeling the scholar, I add, "I know they were introduced to North America in the 1890s and spread all over the continent. The folks who brought them here wanted to introduce one of each of the bird species mentioned in Shakespeare's writings."

"Have you ever seen a ginormous flock of them?"

"No more than a hundred or so."

"We're going to Wales today to witness a murmuration of starlings."

"Murmuration?"

"Picture a massive flock of starlings, say several hundred thousand, all flying together as if guided by a single mind. Their behavior in murmuration is unlike any other birds in the world. When one starling in the flock changes direction or speed, all the other birds respond. They do so nearly simultaneously regardless of the size of the flock. When you watch them and think of the infinite mind, you will wonder if they share one mind—that for a few moments, they are cells of one living organism."

Always ready for adventure, I spring to my feet. "Let's go."

Holly takes my hand. "Picture two hundred thousand birds flying together. Close your eyes and count to ten."

When I reach ten, I open my eyes. We are standing on a bluff overlooking vast wheat fields and green pastures. In the distance, a small mountain range appears to be superimposed silhouettes of differing shades of gray. It's late afternoon, the sun is shining, and the air, hazy and humid.

"Welcome to Carmarthenshire, Wales. This place provides a lot of the peace and tranquility we promised ourselves earlier."

Something's different, but I'm not sure what. While not moving in slow motion exactly, every creature appears to be taking its time. That tranquility ceases the moment an extraordinary cloud of birds explodes on the scene and flows as if one mind controls its every move.

"This," Holly says, "Is murmuration of starlings."

I observe this immense organism and say nothing. Somehow words don't seem to be sufficient.

Holly squeezes my shoulder. "Tell me what you're feeling."

I catch myself before starting another monologue about what I *think* and repeat Holly's question to myself: *what am I feeling?*

"Let's see, I'm short of breath, but I feel nothing in my gut. The hair on my arms...total goose-flesh. My feelings: awe, wonder, happiness, and more. I respect the unfathomable creativity of the infinite mind for how this murmuration came to exist."

Holly strokes my forearm coaxing the prickly hair to lie down. "For the last few days, you have been deeply cerebral. Today is about letting go and allowing yourself to BE. No thinking, no planning, no wondering. Your mind is to be deliciously quiet, as if you have been meditating for the past year.

"But unlike usual meditation practice, today you will be immersed in the beauty of creation and, if you so choose, celestial music as well."

I zero my awareness on the murmuration. Then, quietly at first, I hear the opening strains of *Pachelbel's Canon in D*. As it crescendos, the murmuration intensifies and becomes more spirited. Buoyed by the music, I merge into the murmuration. I can't pick myself out from the others. I'm just one of a great mass of starlings. I sense Holly at my wingtip. I feel in touch with the six nearest birds and alter my course by cueing on them. I have no perception of the whole. I have no conscious thought of altering my direction. I'm but one cell of a great organism. I'm not responsible for any decisions.

Holly's voice cautions. "Careful, Peter, simply be here now."

"Roger that."

Then, imperceptibly, the murmuration dissolves and I doze.

I emerge from nurturing slumber to discover we are in a jungle. Hot and humid, there is no cool breeze. Dozens of Toucans perch on branches all around. Most are purple, with touches of white, yellow, and scarlet. But their bills demand the most attention. Jettisoning my tendency to think like an ornithologist, I gaze at their vibrant colors, including the most perfect orange ever. Several allow me to approach and touch them. I'm amused by the sounds they make, clicking and clacking; they have no song. A Toucan will never be confused with a Hermit Thrush.

"Come here, Peter. This one has a particularly large beak."

I touch it the same way I would caress Holly's cheek. "I wonder how they can fly. Their beaks must be filled with polystyrene."

Holly smiles, "Don't start thinking too much."

I close my eyes and continue touching. Can I experience color by touch? Can I perceive the color orange with any other sense? I try and it's there in my mind; iridescent orange.

"We have an abundance of opportunities awaiting us today. Any requests?"

"I hope you don't think I'm being too analytical, but can you tell me how this helps my becoming a healer?"

"Sure. Care of mind requires immersing it in every imaginable form of beauty. Mind is not solely nourished by meditation, study, and dialogue. As you know, brain and mind blend together. Nurture mind,...nurture body. And vice versa, of course."

I hold my arm out straight, offering it to serve as a Toucan perch. Two birds squabble for room on my arm until they compromise by facing in opposite directions.

Holly shakes her head and smiles expressing approval for my innovative perch.

For some reason, she seems intent on completing her short lecture. "Take the word *recreation* for example; hyphenate it and you get re-creation. During your time with me, you've had experiences nobody in the material world could ever have. Your mind is being re-wired. Neurologists call it neuroplasticity when describing what happens in the brain. When you return to material reality, you will have a re-created mind. Your task will be re-creating your brain."

"Let me take some time to let this soak in."

"Okay."

"But Holly, you told me this wasn't going to be a thinking day."

"You're right, my mistake. Let's get rid of our thinking caps and move on."

I toss my imaginary thinking cap to the ground.

Holly approves; making the same motion, but with a real mortarboard.

"Remember one of our first experiences when we joined a pod of dolphins?"

"I do."

"I provided scuba gear because I knew you were familiar with it. But it didn't take long before you discarded your gear and became a dolphin."

"Okay..."

"Next stop, New Caledonia."

This time we travel high above the Earth cruising among satellites. The kind of thing that might happen if your brain included a *Google Earth* app.

I don't remember splashing down. But once I regain my moorings, I discover I'm lounging on coral reef—under water. I'm breathing as I would on land. I try to locate Holly when a parrotfish joins me.

"Hey, flyboy, how do ya like being a parrotfish?"

"Holly? You're a parrotfish?"

I try to see my body but with eyes situated on either side of my head, it's impossible.

"Don't try to see yourself. Look at me and it will be just like looking in a mirror."

"How can I tell if you're a boy or a girl?"

"You can't. Don't even bother. We're here to visit a great barrier reef in a way no human has before."

I remember parrotfish when I was scuba diving. I've watched as they crunched on hard coral.

"Hey, Holly, want to join me crunching on some coral."

"Go for it. I've never been a fan of eating coral, myself."

I start crunching. "Look here. Coral's not so bad if you're a parrotfish. The little coral cells taste like . . ."

Holly warns me, "Don't tell me they taste like chicken."

"No, they actually taste like sushi."

The colors, shapes and movements are unmatched in the world and when swimming by the power of imagination, words don't suffice to describe the experience.

Holly comes close to me. "Let's do a tail chase, like you used to do in the Marines."

I love tail chases. When flying, one plane would be the bogey and the other, the pursuer. The object is for the bogey to get away using aerobatic procedures. The object of the pursuer is to hang in there and not be shaken-off.

"I'll be the bogey, Peter, see if you can keep up"

With a flip of her tail she disappears. I don't mean she vanishes, rather, she swims out of sight in a microsecond.

"Holly, where'd you go?"

I swim around the coral looking for movement or a parrotfish under a rock. Back when I was really flying, the term we used when looking for—but not finding—the bogey was *no joy*.

Several minutes pass. No joy. Then I feel something nudging my right pectoral fin. Knowing I can't turn my head, I flip end for end and bump beaks with Holly. She smirks, "Couldn't keep up, huh?"

"No, I guess not. Could we try that again, but not at warp speed?"

"Sure, what do you say we just amble along and take in the beauty?"

"Works for me."

As we cruise, I see why Holly picked New Caledonia; the coral isn't bleached like so many other reefs. We swim from shallow to deep, both hugging the reef and moseying out to sea.

"I have a question, Holly. Who eats us?"

She turns quickly so we're beak to beak. "Nobody."

"A parrotfish has a pretty good life. In my next life, I could come back as a parrotfish."

"Are you ready for your next adventure?"

"Sure enough. Fly me to the moon, if you like."

*Poof.*

I'm among a herd of white goats grazing in a lush mountain meadow. Many have copper bells around their necks that clatter as they move. I don't see any people, but a very large white dog approaches. He appears curious and a little aggressive.

"Can you guess where we are. Peter?"

"The mountains, green fields, the herd of sheep...my guess, Switzerland?"

"You win!" With that, she hands me a dark chocolate bar.

Before I can unwrap the chocolate, a Great Pyrenes sniffs my hand. I greet him tentatively, "Hello . . ."

He offers a paw to shake. Very unusual behavior for a livestock guard dog. They are usually suspicious and stand-offish.

"What's your name, boy?"

"My name is Ingrid, and I'm not a boy, you bozo."

I watch her smelling my chocolate. "Do you want a bite?"

"Are you clueless? Dogs aren't supposed to eat chocolate. It's poison to us. I was checking to see if there were any almonds."

I look around for Holly, but at the moment, she's AWOL again.

Ingrid turns, looking back over her herd. Her head bobs, as if she's counting. "Excuse me, I've got to make sure none of my charges has wandered off."

Many years ago, I raised dairy goats. Pick up a baby goat, sit on a hay bale, and cuddle it until it falls asleep. Pure serenity.

Ingrid must see something's amiss. She returns to the herd at a fast trot. I follow, but don't attempt to keep up. When I do come to the first baby goat, I pick it up, and cradle it to my chest. Sure enough. In less than a minute, its head is resting on my shoulder. I slow my pace till I stop, and slowly rock side to side, just like I rocked my infant sons a long time ago.

Those were moments when all was right with the world. I didn't dwell on problems or conflicts. It was time when my relationship with my boys was without flaw.

I feel a touch on my shoulder. "Whatcha got there?"

"I got a baby."

"You look pretty content. How long has it been since you've done that?"

"More than thirty years."

"Why so long? You appear to be as peaceful as the sleeping kid."

"I don't know for sure. I guess I got too busy."

Holly responds, "Uh-huh. Too busy."

"That's the way I've lived most of my life. I remember a saying I came across a long time ago: *Death is nature's way of getting you to slow down.*"

I recall a Simon and Garfunkel tune, *The 59TH Street Bridge Song.* It starts with the phrase, *slow down, you move too fast.*"

Holly whispers, "Make that your song—your personal anthem."

I recall another group who recorded it, *Harper's Bizarre.* I used to play it on a cassette in my car stereo, a long time ago.

As we look across the herd, Holly remarks, "They're all white."

"They're called Saanens. I competed against them at goat shows. They're thought to be the best milk producers. But my favorites were Toggenburgs, brownish-gray color with white markings. I thought they were more personable. They looked me in the eyes. We connected just like dogs and humans."

Holly takes my face in her hands. "Look at you, Peter Andresen, you're in an imaginary meadow in Switzerland and you're talking to me about dairy goats. How is your stress level at the moment?"

"Less than absolute zero."

Ingrid returns from her mission. "I see you're still here."

She takes a moment to scratch behind one ear. "Let me tell you about duty. As a Livestock Guard Dog, I'm with my flock twenty-four hours a day, seven days a week, three hundred sixty-five days a year. I'll give my life for any one of them. They *are* the reason I exist."

I think back on Jesse's teaching about shepherds and sheep. I bet they had dogs helping as well. I wish they had mentioned them in the Bible.

Holly seems a little antsy. "We would stay and talk longer, but we have one more stop."

Ingrid stands up on her back legs, places her paws on Holly's shoulders and proceeds to give her big soggy-tongue kiss the length of Holly's face. When Ingrid sits, I kneel, throw my arms around her neck, and grip her coarse fur. I revel in the scents of woodland meadows, baby goats, and wet dog.

Next instant, we're back flying among the satellites.

"What's our last stop?"

Black screen.

Once again, I try to get my bearings. I think I'm somewhere in the Himalayas. I remember seeing these mountains when we visited Shangri La. Holly's not here. I'm alone in a cave with a fire before me. Someone has wrapped me in a wool blanket.

I breathe and that's all.

I BE.

# CHAPTER 15
## LUCY 07

B LACK. ALL I see is black. Not a hint of light...anywhere.
I have no idea what time it is. Or what day. I do recall
Holly and I took the most amazing trip a few days ago.

The bedsheets are tangled around my legs. I hear waves lapping on the beach which helps to soothe my restlessness. My stale mouth hasn't had a bite to eat or drink since dinner. I'm alone in my room. Some nights Holly and I don't sleep together. I don't know why, we just don't.

A voice in my mind starts goading me, "Get up, Marine. Get going. You gotta fly today."

Dressed in my skivvies, I leave the rumpled bed and venture into the living room faintly illuminated by a single votive candle. I murmur, "Holly . . ." If she's sleeping, I don't want to wake her.

"I'm right behind you."

Her nude body molds to my back. We turn and enfold one another with a long, sensuous hug.

"You're up early. Isn't this the hour Marines call 'zero-dark-thirty?'"

"Strange, you would say that. A couple of minutes ago I heard a voice tell me I had to fly today."

Holly's reply surprises me, "You do have to fly today.

"I do?"

She heads into the kitchen. "First, let me start a fire and brew some coffee."

I mutter to myself, "I gave up flying after the Gulf War. It was not a good time for me."

Wrapped in a light blue housecoat, Holly reappears. "Here's your coffee, commander. I found a blueberry Danish, too."

She slides a table next to my chair and curls up on my lap. "Let's snuggle awhile. I fear for you today."

I don't like the sound of that, so I try to switch the mood. "They say laughter is the best medicine, but snuggling is right up there, too."

We embrace, and sway back and forth, pausing for leisurely kisses.

I attempt another diversion. "Hey, Holly, I remember a tune from a long time ago; something about begging General Custer to not make a soldier go to the Little Bighorn to fight with those Indians."

Holly smiles, but I detect darkness in her expression. "Peter, we need to talk about black holes. Specifically, your black hole. Seems fitting since it's pitch dark outside."

I place my cup on the floor. Hot coffee and my dry mouth don't go well together.

Holly's face darkens. "Don't answer these questions; just listen. Why don't you practice medicine anymore? Why did you go bankrupt? Why do you remain depressed despite therapy and drugs? Why no girlfriends since Annie? Why almost no friends at all?"

"I try not to think about stuff like that."

"Why?"

"Despite prayer, drugs, and therapy, I've stayed stuck. So I finally decided to make the best of my situation and live out my remaining days."

"How's that working for you?"

"Can't say I'm doing very well. Of course, there's also Parkinson's."

Holly furrows her brow, "I recall during some of your self-assured moments, you've described PD as a gift or even a teacher. You can't have it both ways. Is Parkinson's a blessing or a curse?"

My jaw clenches. Is Holly breaking the spell? "What's with you? Are you becoming my grand inquisitor?"

"Part of your mind is trapped. Until today, your experiences here have been positive, even fun. But, I'm sorry, that will not the case today."

For the first time, I feel angry at Holly. "What are you saying? Are we done? Finished?"

"No. But there's a black hole inside you so massive, light cannot escape. It's not subject to my influence. You're going to have to face it without me."

The ready-room at Shaikh-Isa Air Base, Bahrain, is identical to the one back at Cherry Point: whiteboards and giant TV screens at the front; windows along one side look down on the flight line; and blessed air conditioning always turned just a little too cold. The bottomless coffee urn is half-full with burnt coffee, while sweet roll scraps litter the counter and nearby floor.

Self-assured flight crews guffaw and trade insults. But, everything becomes silent the second our CO enters.

"Attention on deck!"

We snap-to until our CO says, "As you were." Then he motions for us to take our seats.

We address Lieutenant Colonel F. G. Carter as Sir, Skipper, or Colonel. When he's not around, we're apt to call him *Fox-Golf* Carter—his initials, F. G., using the NATO phonetic alphabet.

The room remains silent as we find our seats: front rows for majors and captains; back rows for lieutenants and warrant officers. I'm the odd man out. Technically, I'm a Lieutenant Commander in the Navy. The Marines don't have a medical corps, so they fill that need by co-opting Navy personnel. While I fly in the Bombardier-Navigator's (BN) seat, I'm not a NATOPS Certified BN. I'm the squadron flight surgeon. I don't know how to operate the avionics needed for night or IFR missions, but I do a good job with visual ordinance delivery and close air support.

"Okay, gentlemen, listen up. I want to remind you General Moore has accomplished what the First Marine Air Wing couldn't during Vietnam: we are not playing second fiddle to the Air Force."

Everyone claps, cheers and exchanges high-fives.

"That means if we screw up, we can't blame it on anyone but ourselves. It also means if we kick ass, we claim the glory.

"Today we'll fly close air support. We'll go out in two plane gaggles, so before you leave the ready-room, pick your wingman. When we approach our targets, we'll be flying close to the deck. You know what that means: if they have any surviving Triple-A, you could be toast. But the CO of HMLA-269 says his Sea Cobras kicked ass and took no prisoners. Our greatest threat will be small arms fire."

Despite groaning from the crews, he continues, "Each aircraft will have a MER under each wing armed with twelve Mark 81, 250-pound bombs. If you find enemy troops in the open, use the two Mark 77 napalms on your centerline. You'll have two cannisters."

After briefings on the weather and maps showing where friendlies are located, the meeting breaks up.

Pointing at me, our XO, Major Pudge Cummings announces in the fashion of a comedic narrator of a farce, "I'll take the quack, somebody has to stick with that squid. I want to make sure he returns safely."

Every crew member has a handle—a nickname used for casual reference or teasing. All flight surgeons are named Quack. Squid is not my handle; it is a *term of endearment* Marines use to describe anybody in the Navy.

Major Cummings has more poundage around his middle than a Marine should. His first name is Gerald—a name no one uses if they know what's good for them. His handle is Pudge or XO. The two of us have flown a dozen missions together. Back at Cherry

Point our families did a lot together. He owned a boat and water skis, so we took our brides and kids out on the Neuse River to have fun. Over our time together, Pudge and I managed to drink enough beer to cure our alcohol deficiency.

Once on the flight line, we don our torso harness, anti-G suit, and helmet. My crew chief, Staff Sergeant Joyce Bennett, straps me in and connects my anti-G suit, oxygen mask, and communications cable. In her mind, the aircraft belongs to her. She looks like an NFL linebacker and is one hundred percent professional, but mixes just enough kidding to be real.

Our helmets are padded to protect our hearing; so she shouts, "You're all set, Doc. Anything else I can do for you?"

I shake my head and give her a thumbs-up.

She shakes her index finger back at me, "You bring my aircraft back in its current condition or there'll be hell to pay."

Before she steps down, we exchange sloppy salutes. Minutes later, our crew hooks us to an APU and Pudge fires up the twin Pratt-Whitneys and we're ready to roll.

"You ready, Doc?"

"Yes, sir."

"Arm your seat and stop that 'sir' shit, or I'll make sure your next deployment is on a sub-tender in the North Atlantic."

I respond with my best Bill Murry impersonation, "Ejection seat armed...Pudge."

With that, we take our place third in line and soon head down the runway. Besides being ugly, the A6 rumbles like a worn-out cattle truck. In twenty seconds, we're airborne. Two minutes later we're cruising four hundred miles an hour on our way to ten thousand feet.

"Well, Doc, this is your twentieth mission. How many have been in the face of enemy fire?"

"About half."

"That could be the case today, too. Small arms fire has shot down many an aircraft. When I flew in Nam, I know two guys who were shot down that way. Fortunately, they both made it out."

VMA 224's call word is Lucy. Each aircraft is assigned a number. Our wingman's callsign is Lucy 02. Ours is Lucy 07. Twenty minutes into the flight, Pudge gets on the horn, "Lucy 02, time to get down and dirty. The quack and I will take the lead. Stay at our nine o'clock and follow us."

"Roger that, Lucy 07."

Looking at our ALQ display, I take comfort there isn't any enemy radar painting us. Ground fire should be our only concern.

"Hey, Doc, what's that on the ground at our two o'clock?"

"I'm not sure. Let's take a closer look."

Radar altimeter says we're flying five hundred feet above the deck.

"Hey, Pudge, it looks like a tank that bit the dust."

We circle to come from a different direction. Still no joy; just a burned-out pile of scrap metal.

Pudge radios, "Lucy 02, nobody's home. Let's keep hunting. Maybe better if we look around a little higher...say a thousand feet."

"Roger that."

We visit two more metal corpses; nobody's home at either one.

"Well, Doc, looks like we're all dressed up with no place to go?"

"Looks like it."

We climb and level off at a thousand feet, then kick back and shoot the bull. "How's it going, Andy, you gonna make the Marine Corps a career?"

"I doubt it. First of all, the Navy owns me, body and soul, so it's not likely they'll let me remain a jarhead. And I'm planning on specializing; just not sure in what. How about you? What's your future looking like?"

"I've nearly got twenty years under my belt. Next assignment, or the one after it, I'll take my turn as CO."

"How's your bride feel about you going for thirty?"

"She's okay with it, but she'd really like to settle down in one place. My little sister just lost her husband to cancer. She's going to come and live with us when I return."

"I didn't know you had a sister."

"She's eleven years younger than me and has her shit together. She'll be in our home by the end of the . . ."

"WHAT THE FUCK!"

A half-dozen Roman candles blaze across our canopy.

"Triple A!" Pudge shouts. He dives, demanding Lucy 07 give us everything she's got. We level off at a hundred feet.

"Did you see where they came from?"

Just then Lucy 02 screams, "Lucy 07, I'm hit."

"How bad?"

"Flight controls seem okay, but we got a hydraulic leak somewhere."

"Any fire?"

"No lights. Don't smell anything."

Pudge's tone becomes that of a warm-hearted football coach. "Let's get out of here and climb to angels twenty. I'll hang at your six; give you a look-see."

But before we change course, more Roman candles shoot by—this time from our six. Lucy 07 lurches and shudders.

Pudge hollers, "We're hit!"

Lucy 02 comes back, "How bad?"

Pudge doesn't answer. He's trying to make sense of our dashboard that's lit up like a pinball machine. He cuts back the power and resumes level flight. A few lights flicker and go off. No more Roman candles.

"How's it look?" I ask.

"Had a fire warning light, but it's gone out."

Our ALQ beeper interrupts, telling us a fire-control radar is painting us. Pudge dumps four wads of chaff, hits full military power and starts a six-G turn to starboard. "Just let me see those mother-fucking camel jockeys!"

Fighting to stay conscious at six-Gs I activate the ordinance panel. "I thought the Cobras took out the triple-A."

Pudge calls, "Lucy 02, report."

"I think we can make it back. Should I jettison my ordinance?"

"You see anything you can drop it on? Let's take a quick look."

Our tight turn already has our wings perpendicular to the ground. From the cockpit, the horizon looks vertical

Lucy 02 squawks, "Holy fuck, XO, look down there. Looks like ants pouring out of an anthill."

From hidden bunkers, hundreds of Iraqi troops spread out, fleeing in all directions. But we won't hit anything if we drop our bombs now.

"I think we're okay for the moment, Doc. Let's find some sand monkeys and dump our napes."

"Sure you want to do that? Our wings are anything but level."

"I don't give a shit. We didn't come all this way just to get shot down. We've got a chance to fry a bunch of crispy critters."

I rig the ordinance panel so the napalm will automatically arm five seconds after release. I check the altimeter, we're at five hundred feet. "Pudge, we need to go down a little more. We should drop the napes at a hundred feet or so to get the most bang for the buck."

"Gotcha, Doc."

The concept behind napalm is to spread the flaming gel across the ground and cover the greatest area possible. Pudge softens the G load so the cannisters will deploy safely

I call "Pickle" and Pudge releases the napes.

Seconds later the napalm canisters start their deadly descent. But no sooner than they're gone, the dashboard lights flash red and orange and the cabin fills with smoke. A computer-generated voice orders, "Eject, eject, eject!"

"Jettison the MERs, Doc."

Pudge blows the canopy. The ensuing tempest blasts the smoke from our open cockpit.

"Eject, Doc!"

I pull the face-curtain ejection activator. The Martin-Baker canon punches my butt with a twelve G blow.

Though we didn't plan to, we ejected parallel to the ground. Barely enough time for our ejection seats to separate and our chutes to deploy.

I look for Pudge, but all I see is Lucy 07 exploding. I twist around and stretch my neck.

*Where's Pudge? His chute?*

Nowhere...nothing...

The A6's parachute canopy was designed a little too small for landing on solid ground. It was okay over water. I hit the ground hard, skip a couple times, and black-out.

*What happened? Where am I?*

As I try to answer, my vision clears. Looking down at me is an old gray-bearded Arab holding an AK-47. He looks like he's starving.

I reach into my torso harness pocket to retrieve my ID booklet. I open it to the page showing a red cross and the word, MEDIC. The facing page has a red crescent and the word, MEDIC in six languages.

The man grabs my card and studies it. In the process, he drops his weapon but makes no effort to pick it up. I know if I tried, I'd be dead in seconds. As more gaunt troops gathers, I'm shocked; they're all malnourished, unshaven, and old. For sure, they are not members of the Republican Guard.

As they talk and gesticulate, a chorus of distant voices fills the air screaming in agony.

Two guys pull me to my feet. My back feels like a cross-cut saw is hard at work. I wipe my back to check for blood. My hand come back clean. The ejection must have fractured a vertebrae.

*Can I feel my feet? Yeah, I can. Good.*

The crowd presses in, shaking fists and punching me; their voices raised with unintelligible shrieking.

*Is this how I die?*

Someone kicks my feet out from under me. On the ground, I curl into a defensive fetal position while being kicked, punched, and cursed. I don't know how long it continued. My mind floated above the scene. I watch the torture, but feel nothing.

*Where's Pudge?*

A sudden burst from an AK-47 silences the crowd.

Back in my body, I become aware the blows have ceased. I venture to peek at what's happening. Two younger, muscular men sporting well-trimmed back beards approach. The old man hands them my documents. They study them for a moment and then one kneels beside me and speaks in broken English. "You, a doctor? Why you bomb us?"

"I can't answer that question. Ask the Marine Corps. I'm just following orders."

I straighten my body to lie on my back, the better to see him. He punches my face, crushing my nose. I gasp, choking on the blood streaming down my throat. I turn my head to spit as the crowd presses harder and starts kicking me again. My mind returns to its uninvolved-observer place overhead.

The other officer shouts to quiet the crowd. He speaks to the man who broke my nose—I think they're officers in the Republican Guard. The broke-my-nose guy must be a lower rank. He talks less and constantly nods his head. He looks down at me with infinite contempt and spits in my face. Then, he draws a small scimitar from his belt and holds the point beneath my chin.

"I have good news. You going to live." He grins with eternal hatred. "But you will live with a curse. So bad, you will beg Allah, The Merciful, to die. End your suffering."

I don't respond. I'm transfixed with his Satanic face.

They haul me back to my feet. Satan grabs my hair forcing me to look at the wailing charred bodies spread across the landscape. The napalm found its target.

"See those men? My men. They die. We have no medicine. They must be killed. End their suffering."

Grabbing a fistful of my hair, he forces my chin to the tip of his dagger. "We give you job. To live, you cut their throats; finish your evil attack."

I feel like my head will burst. "I can't do that!"

"No, you must." He places the scimitar blade on my little finger. "If you no do, I cut off your fingers. Each time you no kill. I cut off finger, one at a time. Then, we cut your belly open. Vultures feast on you before you die."

He forces the dagger handle into my hand and pulls me stumbling to the nearest man, his burned skin peeling off in sheets. "Here, doctor, first patient. End suffering now."

I became a robot. I slash the burn victim's throat from ear to ear, making sure to sever his trachea and both carotid arteries with one violent motion. It takes about ten seconds for him to die. He tries to mouth words, but can't utter a sound.

"Oh, doctor, you good surgeon. Now, look around. You pick next patient. Get moving or I chop-chop your fingers."

I wish I had a god to beseech. I try to pray the way I remember, "Please, Jesus, take this cup from me."

I wait for an answer until Satan pokes me in my ass with his AK. "Pray to Allah, the Giver of Justice, but he won't listen. No. He send you to Lake of Fire."

*Your radio, Andresen. Turn it on so the choppers can hear what's happening.*

I purposely stumble over the next body and fall on my face. I switch my radio on and mute it. Satan is too busy beseeching Allah to notice what I'm doing.

My next *patient* couldn't be eighteen years old; more like fifteen. He's bawling, but his burns aren't extensive. He moves his legs well. I don't see any broken bones.

"This boy should not die," I try to stick to simple words. "Too good, too strong."

I grab the boy's head and pull his cheek next to mine. I draw my finger by our throats in a slashing motion. "No cut. He live."

Apparently Satan understands. He looks the boy over. "You right. No kill."

Gritting my teeth and begging forgiveness from all gods everywhere, I proceed to kill the next three victims, making sure I complete the job with a single violent slash. I know if I'm brutal enough, the deep slash will shorten their suffering.

I select my next victim. This one is nearly dead. His tongue hangs from the side of his mouth. He's unconscious; the easiest one so far.

The next two must be friends. While they are screaming with pain, they make furtive attempts to comfort the other one at the same time. By now, the blood clotting on my hands makes it harder to hold the knife. When I start the first one, the knife slips from my hands. I only manage to sever the trachea but not the carotids. When I search in the fist-deep blood, I don't find anything.

The second guys comes up with the knife, but doesn't attack me. Instead, he completes cutting his friend's arteries. I'm paralyzed at what I see. The second man stuns me, handing me the knife and gesturing he wants me to slash his throat. I don't waste a second and slash his throat ear-to-ear.

Just then Satan jumps to his feet; the same time I hear helicopters coming. Men who are able start fleeing in panic. I fumble to unmute my mic. I look up just in time to see Satan rushing at me, scimitar in hand. I try to run, but my back hurts so much, I only stumble. When he nearly reaches me, I tuck my chin to my sternum so slashing my throat won't be so easy.

The sound of approaching choppers and fifty caliber machine guns firing cause Satan to stand for a moment and look that direction. As he does, I kick his feet from under him. I roll several times until the barrel of an AK-47 on the ground strikes my chest.

I grab it, cycle the action, and empty the clip on Satan. It's over so fast. I fall back exhausted but relieved.

Then everything turns black.

Holly rocks me in her arms while stroking my cheeks. I don't speak. I feel paralyzed. My brain is frozen. She speaks softly in my ear. "No person can live with those tragic memories. Now you've purged your black hole, I'm covering it. If you access those tragic events again, you will be able to do so, but you will not experience any feelings. This type of healing makes it possible to remember, but not-reexperience tragic events."

# CHAPTER 16
# THE APP

FOR THE MOMENT It's like yesterday never happened
Dom Perignon for breakfast again and the best crepes
ever. I never feel too full. Squeezing my waist, I appreciate I'm
looking more buff—despite eating all I want and just hanging
out.

This morning though, I'm bored. How is it possible to experience boredom in paradise? I wondered about that when I was
little. The heaven I pictured was all clouds, harps, and going to
church. I wondered if hell would have more interesting people
and if I could get used to the heat.

"Holly, how many days have I been hanging out here and just
being lazy?"

Holly is busy trimming the flowers next to the porch. "It's
been a week. Why do you ask?"

"Lying around in paradise is actually getting a little boring. I
feel something's missing."

"Like what?"

"I dunno. Maybe a job? Maybe a sense of purpose? I used to
get antsy on vacations. I found I needed my cell phone so I could
connect with work—what I used to call reality."

Putting down her clippers, Holly joins me on the porch. "How
are you feeling about last week?"

"I feel okay. But I don't understand why I've been so sluggish.
Wasn't that big of a deal."

"You think not?"

"No. Of course, getting shot down was a bummer, but the rescue choppers found Pudge and me. I'll never know why they sent me to Germany to repair my nose and kept me in the hospital for months?"

I down another healthy swallow of Dom nectar.

"What gets me is I never found out where Pudge moved. I remember just before the shooting started; he was telling me about his little sister. Despite being eleven years apart, they were very close. He told me her husband just died of cancer and she was going to move to North Carolina to live with his wife, Jenny. Why in hell did they send me to Germany? I wanted to stay with Pudge and my squadron."

I clench my fist and hit my thigh. "And that son-of-a-bitch never answered any of my letters. It was then I decided that squadron loyalty didn't amount to a bucket of pig swill. Fuck 'em."

Holly bites her lip. "You're not quite finished yet. How do you *feel* about your experiences in Desert Storm?"

"Confused."

"How so?"

"I mean, I earned an Air Medal. Big deal. The Purple Heart for my broken nose was a bit much. But to this day, I can't understand the Bronze Star. Were they just handing them out for the hell of it? The document says it was for valor in the face of the enemy. What enemy? I never met an enemy face-to-face."

Holly doesn't answer my question. "Remember how you've always had such a heavy heart; how you've always carried a cloak of darkness?"

"Yeah, so?"

"How's your heavy heart today? Your dark cloak?"

I stand and start pacing. *What's the big deal here?*

"C'mon, Holly, let's forget it."

"Close your eyes, Peter. Take your time and look deep inside. What's there? Has anything changed?"

*Strange...when I focus on my heart, it does feel lighter. I mean different. It's like heavy bands used to constrict it, but the bands have disappeared. My heart has all the room it needs. Breathing is easy. I can exhale.*

Holly smiles. "Some people say it's like being born."

I open my eyes. "I notice you didn't say, *born again.*"

She stifles a giggle. "We're not talking about that, silly guy. We're talking about how you feel—right here, right now."

I deliberately exhale. And then repeat it several times.

"How do I feel? Light as a helium balloon, free to go wherever a breeze takes me."

"What about the black cloak?"

Closing my eyes again, I descend to the center of my deepest feelings. Something *is* different. A comforting warmth, almost fluidlike, fills me from head to toe. "I feel warm inside."

"And?"

"I don't need the cloak anymore."

I open my eyes and smile at my angel-genie. "Something's different in my mind. But for some strange reason, I don't think I need to know why or how it happened."

Holly throws her arms around my neck. "Sweet Peter. Your curse was never about Parkinson's. It was caused by a malignant black presence in your mind; a beast named, depression, also known as PTSD. Your Parkinson's is a completely separate matter."

Laughing, I lift Holly until her toes can't touch the floor and whirl her around as if we're playful lovers in a romantic movie. "Put me down," she laughs. "We need to talk about today."

"What if I don't want to?"

"Because your time is almost over and there are still critical lessons you must learn."

I stop and let her down.

Her knitted brow belies something deeper coming my way. "Let's go for a walk. I'll bring snacks and a bottle of wine."

Soon, we're ambling along the beach just as we did when we first met. We continue to walk holding hands but saying nothing.

When we come upon a grove of palm trees where there's plenty of shade, she drops my hand. "Let's plant ourselves here."

We stretch out and savor a 1984 vintage Grand Cru Chablis while nibbling bites of goat cheese and crackers.

Holly still appears serious and I'm beginning to feel fidgety. "Okay, my sweet genie-angel, what's up for me today?"

"You understand we are nearing the end of your time here. Today, your final guide is going to purge your mind of all unnecessary science and philosophy. He will install the *placebo app* into your brain."

I scrunch my lips. "Oh, is that all?"

"Notice, I said *brain*, not *mind*."

"You mean the computer in my skull; the organ which will cease functioning when I die"

"Precisely. Since your arrival, you've had several different guides. Which one would you like to do the honors?"

The word 'Solomon' flashes before my eyes.

Holly claps, "Perfect, Peter, just perfect!"

I'm looking over a grassy meadow when I hear a voice, "Good to see you again."

I wheel around and see an enormous raven. Unlike other ravens, this one is gold.

"Solomon, is that you?"

"Indeed, it is."

"But, you're so...gold."

"I thought I'd gussy up for the occasion."

"What occasion?"

"Before you return, we need to simplify your message so it can be grasped by anyone. You will teach people how to induce their own placebo response. We're not talking about cure. While everybody would love to be cured, they will be grateful to have symptoms put on hold or reversed"

"Just how, pray tell, is that going to happen?"

"I'm taking you to meet your placebo manager."

"Placebo manager?"

"Yes, you will have an app installed in your brain."

I lift my eyebrows. "I'm not sure I understand, but I'm game to continue."

Solomon looks me up and down. "Put on your raven body and let's go."

I imagine I'm flying. Soon, we're wingtip to wingtip soaring over a great expanse of open land; not a dwelling or person in sight.

"Behold, Peter, the Earth without humankind."

Open plains, rolling hills, majestic mountains, forests, lakes, rivers, and streams stretch as far as I can see. There are no structures, no roads, no airplanes, but instead, an abundance of birds and animals. *This must be Eden.*

"Indeed," Solomon responds. "Humankind, the species with the most advanced brains inherited this. Soon it will be destroyed. Gone until another evolution replaces it; hopefully with creatures capable of empathy for all creation."

"Is that what our future holds?" I feel like Scrooge pleading with the ghost of Christmas's-yet-to-come.

Flying leisurely along, Solomon answers, "There is one gift not available to those of us who inhabit the world of imagination. It is knowing the future. I speak from accumulated wisdom, not prescience."

"I'm glad I'm alive now; not during the span of my grandchildren's lives. I fear those years will manifest our worst nightmares."

Solomon flies on in silence.

"What can I do?"

"If you present your message so people can learn from it, you may bring about a new understanding of the mind and maybe even the infinite mind. But you must be watchful of how you express yourself, or people may think you're introducing another religion."

Now it's my turn to fly in silence

After a while, Solomon starts a gradual descent. "Soon, we'll arrive at Shangri La. I understand you've been there before."

Landing beside the pool where Holly and I stopped, Solomon takes time to arrange his gold plumage. I walk to the pool to look at my reflection.

*Oh my God! My feathers are gold, too.*

After drinking from the pool, Solomon points to half of a gymnast's parallel bars. "Let's perch."

I join him and discover a bag holding fresh-cut red meat.

Sounding gleeful, Solomon says, "Oh good. They prepared dinner for us. This is so much better than fighting with other scavengers to grab a bite of some decaying carcass."

I find I can balance on one foot while using the other to steady a bite of meat. "Look at what I can do, Solomon."

"Looks like you've got the hang of this."

"Having changed bodies often enough, I've developed the knack of adapting to whatever creature I am at the time."

We finish our fixins. I watch how methodically Solomon preens his feathers and then I proceed to do the same. Next, I fluff my feathers and let them lie down in perfect order.

After a good meal, I'm ready to continue. "Okay, so what's next for me?"

"Get comfortable. I'm going to go over information we've touched on during your visit."

I relax and settle down very carefully making sure my breast feathers cover my feet.

"When you arrived this last time, we knew you had potential, but we also knew you might not be up to the task. You confirmed your readiness to return to the material world by how you came through your last event."

"That wasn't such a big deal."

"I know in your mind, it wasn't. But to the infinite mind, it proved you are ready to bear whatever load may be required."

"I don't get it."

"When your appendix was removed, did you know what happened?"

"No, of course not. I was only ten years old, plus I was asleep."

"How long did it take to recover?"

"About six weeks. At least that's what Dr. Ingalls told my mom."

"How long did it take you to recover from your last event?"

"Holly said it was about a week, but I didn't get operated on this time."

"Actually, Peter, it has been two months. We decided to wait until your mind was fully restored before we told you the truth. What you went through that day in Iraq was far more serious than your appendix surgery."

"What was removed?"

"Darkness."

"Interesting, Holly said the same thing."

Solomon's voice befits the wisest person in history; it is soft, measured, and spoken so clearly I absorb every word. "With Nora, you learned evil is not incarnate, but a manifestation of free minds retelling stories until they all believe a lie. Overcoming evil isn't about vanquishing an entity, it comes with education devoid of misleading myths."

"Misleading myths?"

"Myth is a critical step for developing civilizations. It represents something, the reality of which will become clear with the ongoing evolution of human consciousness. Misleading myths are held by dogmatic minds. They are believed to be factual, not metaphorical."

"I'm beginning to understand."

Solomon ruffles his wings and takes flight. I follow like a well-mannered dog, trusting we will arrive at the right place—wherever that might be.

The sun inches towards the western horizon. Trees are in full autumn dress; my favorite time of year. I recognize this place, it's the oak forest bordering USMC Air Station, Cherry Point. I follow Solomon and land among thousands of oak trees. Not mighty oaks, these are middle-aged trees standing less than a hundred feet tall. Fallen acorns carpet the forest floor. We land and without warning, I become human once more. I step and feel the crunching acorns beneath my feet. I look for Solomon, but only catch a glimpse of a golden raven clearing nearby trees.

"Farewell, Peter. I know your teaching will inspire countless people; some with disabilities, some without."

He flies out of sight before I can respond. Instead, I whisper, knowing he will hear me. "Farewell to you, bearer of untold wisdom."

Every autumn, hundreds of wood ducks pause here to feast on the millions of acorns. Their flocks fly in before sunset. First, a single male zips through, whistling once. He returns, flying straight through again; this time emitting more whistling calls. A few minutes later, scores of wood ducks are everywhere. They fly like slalom racers skiing, twisting and turning, in and out, up and down; even performing end-over-end flips. Their aerobatics would be the envy of every A6 pilot alive. I wonder how many people have witnessed something like this. I'm certain it is very few.

Hands in my pockets, I scuff the acorns. It's like I'm waiting for Gadot. I don't recall the name of my placebo manager, but one name elbows its way into my mind, Proteus.

"Do I hear someone calling my name?"

I can't identify who's speaking. The voice sounds like it's coming from the ground beneath my feet. I look down, but see nothing.

"Is anyone here?"

"You're walking all over me, buddy-boy. Get back. You're damaging my protoplasm. And I'd be much obliged if you address me by my name, Proteus."

"Proteus?"

"You got a problem with that?"

His voice is strange; sounds as if the speaker's vocal cords are slippery, like limp spaghetti.

"I don't see you, Proteus."

"Stop walking all over my protoplasm, dammit. You know, amoebas have feelings too."

*To tell the truth, I never gave it a thought.*

"What do you mean, amoeba?"

"To quote Wikipedia, I'm 'a unicellular organism which has the ability to alter its shape.'"

"But you're supposed to be microscopic."

"For a doctor, you sure don't keep up with microbiology."

"For an amoeba, you've got a big mouth."

"The better to phagocytize you."

*I can't believe I'm arguing with an amoeba.*

"I'm too big to phagocytize."

"You're probably right. I know you've been living pretty high on the hog lately."

"How do you know that?"

"Because we're living in the world of imagination. Did you forget that, dumbass?"

Frustrated, I blurt, "Enough with the back-and-forth already. I'm here to meet some guy to have a special app installed in my brain."

"I'm the one you're looking for, but I'm not *some guy.* I'm Proteus, an intelligent amoeba, for crying out loud."

"Couldn't prove it by me. So far, you're just an invisible blabbermouth."

"Ahem. Let me make myself perfectly clear . . ."

"Good, I'd like that."

"You are still standing on my protoplasm and ripping my cell membrane to shreds. Take ten steps back and give me a few minutes to glue myself together."

I step back, rocking to and fro. "Have it your way. I've got nothing else going on; except brain surgery."

It's still light enough for me to watch the diffuse gelatinous mass start to take shape. It grows taller and rounder. It expands until it looks like a spherical blob of mucus roughly four times the size of a basketball. I still don't see a face or limbs.

"You ready yet?"

The upper pole of the sphere shakes from side to side.

"I guess that means you're not finished?"

The pole shakes back and forth.

I return my attention to the wood ducks. At any given time, a dozen flit about—never a motionless moment. Suddenly, a large winged form flashes into the chaos scattering the wood ducks in an instant. The large winged form; a Northern Goshawk.

By the time I refocus my attention, the Goshawk is on the ground ripping at the body of the one wood duck that didn't get away.

"It happens that way almost every night."

I turn to see Proteus has attained a nearly recognizable form. "Those wood ducks get too focused on food. Hunger and sex make creatures throw caution to the winds."

"Are you finished redesigning yourself?"

"Just a second. I need arms and a face that has eyes, ears, and a mouth. Always thought a nose was a waste of time."

A minute later Proteus is shaped like *Casper, The Friendly Ghost*. But overall, he still reminds me of a clear plastic bag filled with snot.

"Can you do something with your insides? They make me want to barf."

"Very well. I think I'd like to be blue this evening—blue with gold twinkles."

He succeeds. Still shaped like Casper, he's now a deep translucent blue with hundreds of tiny gold stars twinkling inside. His face is a light shade of lavender with huge round eyes and his mouth, a filled-in black circle.

"I see you are a shape-shifter. Can't say I've ever met one."

"There's a lot you don't know about me"

"I'm here to have an app installed in my brain. If you're the man—I mean the amoeba—let's get to it."

"Lie down on your back and close your eyes."

Jelly-like fingers probe my head and all its openings. Proteus, sounding like Louis Armstrong, sings a familiar tune, something about leaving your worries on the doorstep."

Other than his hands and his singing, I sense nothing else.

Proteus makes the sound of a bugle. "Ta Da! All done."

I sit up wondering if anything happened at all. "Is that all?"

"This will activate once you're safely back on Earth."

"How's that gonna happen?"

"It will happen when you see a gold flash from a bird's wing."

"I'm supposed to be on the lookout for canaries?"

Proteus turns and for a minute looks like a stressed out Don Rickles. "Dodo brain, canaries are yellow. Gees!"

"Golden flash...bird's wing?"

Quick as a short-order cook, Proteus wraps his cell membrane around my head and I feel something click in my brain. I wipe off the residual amoeba slime. "What did you just do?"

"I set your app to automatically trigger when you are back home and see the golden flash. Now I won't have to worry about your overrated mammalian brain. Dumb ass."

I ignore his criticism. Imagine being criticized by an oversized amoeba.

Proteus shifts his appearance to sky-blue orb and changes his tone. "You're in for a very dangerous time tomorrow. If this was activated now, while you're still here, you'd most likely become permanently insane on reentry and spend the rest of your life in a mental hospital."

For the first time, Proteus sounds deadly serious.

"Is playtime over?"

"It will be over when you bid Holly farewell tomorrow morning."

*Tomorrow? No, it can't be. We need years, not hours before we say goodbye.*

Proteus sounds like a friend warning me. "Call for transport and go home...now."

# CHAPTER 17
# THE GAUNTLET

I T'S NEARLY DARK when I arrive and deplane from my owl.
For the first time it speaks to me.

"Peter, every time we go anywhere you're asleep. It's part of the
way we do things. After all, we owls are a silent sort and not given
to small talk. Since this is our last flight together, I hope your
reentry will be free from terror."

"Free from terror!"

The bird draws its wing to cover its face. "Oh, dear. Did I just
spill the beans?"

Holly fumes. "Damn right you did. What's your name? I'm
going to report you."

"My name is Hedwig."

"I think I've heard of you. At least your name is familiar."

"When I'm normal sized, I've been a confidant of Harry Pot-
ter."

With nothing left to say, Hedwig shrinks to normal size and
flies away.

Holly and I have been apart all day. Knowing our time
together is drawing to a close, I want to be mindful of every detail
of my beloved genie-angel. I refuse to even consider the word 'terror.' I park the word in my mental cellar and bolt the door.

We treasure our unhurried hug, saying nothing until I totally
relax.

I kiss her, signaling the end of our embrace. "Are we eating on
the beach tonight?"

"We are, but I wasn't sure if you wanted to sit on the ground or something else."

"I get stiff sitting on the ground. I'll opt for a chair."

Holly apparently wants to go all-out. My chair is anything but ordinary, it's a throne.

"You deserve to be *King Peter*, the King of Imaginary Reality. Want me to dress us as if we're medieval royalty?"

"Sure."

Next thing I know, I'm wearing a long purple under-tunic embroidered with gold thread, a light leather outer tunic, a crimson surcoat made of silk, and a hat bedecked with golden pheasant feathers. Holly is less flashy allowing me, like most male birds, to sport fancier plumage.

She nudges my ribs. "How do you like your get-up, your highness?"

"Works for me, but that huge gold throne is too much. How about a double recliner?"

Choosing to forego the throne, we eat few morsels from our banquet. We're not that hungry, so we spend more time cuddling and nuzzling on the recliner. We kiss less often lately, choosing instead to gaze into one another's eyes and lightly caress whatever feels good.

Foregoing discussion, we silently drift into dreamless sleep as her cool fingertips touch my forehead in reassurance.

Blessed repose.

When the first birds announce morning's dawn, I wish I had a snooze button. I don't like how I feel. What's coming? Hedwig mentioned terror. I still lack a Parkinson's tremor, but my anxiety tremor more than makes up for it. My shaky hand makes it difficult, but I manage to unbolt the door to my mental cellar.

A black mamba—must be twelve feet long—raises its evil head to eye level and addresses me; its voice thin and high-pitched. "We will meet for real on your reentry." Then it melts into a small puddle and dries instantly; leaving only a putrid-smelling tar wafer.

Holly is by my side as we study the tar. I know the mamba was not real, but it foresaw an encounter whose outcome could be my demise. Funny how something as innocuous as a small tar remnant can freeze a mind.

"We have less than an hour, my love. So little time to say farewell."

A cold, bottomless fear brings to mind a time when a gun tumbling in a drawer invited me to commit suicide. I'm convinced evil is not incarnate, but after what I just witnessed, I see why the cult of Satan evolved in human minds.

"Take this mamba experience as a warning," Holly says. "Don't let reason give way to fear. Or in neuroscience parlance: don't let your amygdala control your frontal cortex."

I crack a smile. "Why, Holly, you've never spoken to me like that. I mean, like a neuroscientist."

"Until now, I never felt the need."

Unbidden free-associations swirl until one dominates. "I remember the Bible saying something about perfect love driving out all fear."

Holly presses her finger to my lips. "Let me reframe that. True understanding and reason eliminate fear. I know it's not very poetic, but it is true."

As the import of those words grows in my mind, my fear of the black mamba fades...temporarily?

"Peter, the final phase of your training is about take place; solo combat, your personal *mother of all battles*."

I purse my lips and feel my brow squeeze. "I have another question: Where does the infinite mind fit?"

"Good question. Develop your personal schematic of mind and brain. It does not have to be accurate or even true to work. Your brain creates and manipulates symbols all the time. But first . . ."

I watch as she swallows hard and tries to speak, but nothing comes out. She takes my hand and walks me to the porch where coffee, orange juice, and apple turnovers await. Her face is red and swollen. Clenching her jaws, she makes every effort to suppress her tears, but finally yields and falls to the floor weeping.

*My strong, loving genie-angel reduced to this?*

"Holly, I don't want to leave you. Is there no way I can stay?"

She catches her breath and slowly gets to her feet. "Peter, my sweet silly guy, I've never experienced love like ours. Most of my kind experience no feelings at all—let alone a deep and abiding love."

I offer my handkerchief and look for a wristwatch so I know how much time we have. To my surprise, a brand new Fitbit just clicked through six minutes.

Holly seizes my hands with a death-grip. "I have just enough time to brief you before you run the gauntlet."

"Run the gauntlet? That's a lot different than reentry. Isn't it?"

Holly blurts, "Peter, the gauntlet can kill you! Or you could end up spending the rest of your life, a raving schizophrenic in a mental hospital. Honestly, your odds have grown worse because you've come so far."

"I don't understand."

"Because your work seeks to turn human thought away from superstition and towards compassionate understanding. And to understanding there is an infinite mind that will not be manipulated by human thought."

"What about the black mamba?"

"It is the embodiment of fear and ignorance. As such it poses a risk to the very survival of humanity. Never let it be more than an illusion within your mind."

My mouth is so dry my tongue sticks to my teeth.

"What do I need to know?"

"As real as the gauntlet will feel; remember, it's a product of your mind. Your focused mind will win the contest."

BOOM! A sound not unlike *The Hunger Games*.

"One kiss before you go."

Our lips meet and it's like the 4th of July fireworks detonating in my body. Our mouths become one, but just like that, it's over.

"Holly, will I ever see you again?"

"I can't say. We have not been given the gift to foretell the future."

BOOM!

I'm walking on a dry plain. Bare soil complemented by intermittent tufts of withered grass stretch as far as the eye can see. Low gray clouds muffle any sound. And on and on it goes; hour after hour; day after day; month after month; year after year. Alone, empty, I continue walking. I'm fully conscious, but my mind is void.

My back and feet cry for rest. None is granted. Fatigue is infinite. I think each step will be my last, but it isn't. It never is.

A sound, so muffled I cannot hear it, strikes my inner ear neurons. I feel the pulse but there's no sound. Over a long stretch of time—I have no idea how long—the beats grow, merge, and creep into my consciousness. I CAN HEAR!

But what sounds do I hear? My footfalls. My breathing. Not much else, so I continue my desolate journey.

*Am I in Limbo?*

The mere act of asking the question flips some unknown switch. Yes, I have a mind and I have a body. But they're filled with chaos. Loud, throbbing noises pound every cell of my being. I can't muffle them.

A million screaming micro-scimitars shred my brain, my mind, my very existence. The mamba sticks a long black tongue at me and vomits gallons of yellow-green sputum that fills a pool . into which I plunge and sink. It's like being swallowed by a grotesque giant squid. Drowning in putrid slime, I'm propelled through its bowels until defecated onto a pinball table. Instead of flippers striking me, electric eels bite and twist my flesh. I feel pain in every cell.

A dark-bearded man dressed in camouflage clamps one of my hands in a vice while another man uses pruning shears to sever my fingers, one joint at a time. All around, countless burned men wail in agony, begging to die. The men cleaving my fingers cackle and spit in my mouth as I scream.

Two words break through the din; *Infinite mind.*

I affirm my mind exists and is nourished by gold strands of energy coursing throughout the universe from the moment of creation.

Lying on a supportive cloud bank, I'm torment-free for the first time since leaving Holly. I see her beautiful nude body resting on the cloud beside me. Finally, a moment of respite.

But I'm wrong. Holly screams for me to protect her, but I cannot. The python already coiled around her body tightens. Holly's face bulges as the constriction turns it blue and prevents her from making sound. She mouths my name. But I am powerless. I cannot move. I'm unable to speak. With the final tightening of the serpent's constricting body, Holly's head explodes, her brain matter spattering in my face.

*Remember, this is happening in your mind. Only one person can make it stop.*

My mind. Can do.

I imagine I'm flying with Solomon. He's at my wingtip but says, "I can't be here."

With that, he's gone.

I must be entering material reality. I purge my mind of the gore. Most make no sense; especially the finger amputations. Never mind. I realize I can't imagine I'm flying and make it happen. My feet are on the ground. Reminds me of the distinction between *serving* during wartime and having your *boots on the ground.*

I'm walking along a familiar stretch of beach. It's where I met Holly. Gosh darn. I think I'm nearing home, wherever home is.

A voice says, "You're not finished yet,"

I look around but see nothing. "Who are you?"

Silent pause.

"Let me see you."

More silence.

"Then go fuck yourself."

"You're not home yet."

The black mamba slithers and settles into a fighting coil inches from my feet. "You know I've got you now. You let your guard down too soon. You've completed the gauntlet, but not the reentry."

Its thin, high-pitched voice grates my hearing like ice picks piercing glass. Because of its length and power, it moves its head from its ground coil to eye level.

"I will kill you quickly if you confess your girlfriend is a whore that fucks the devil."

I banish the serpent's words from my mind and force myself to look deep into its eyes. Its pupil like its open mouth is pitch black.

"I believe you're the one who is confused. There is no devil, no Satan. It is the product of mistaken human minds."

I feel no fear. I sneer at my adversary. "As I say these very words, you are not evil, you're merely the most deadly snake in the world. And because we have been talking, I know I still retain some of the powers I acquired in imaginary reality."

The mamba widens its hood and hisses.

"You are imaginary. I am alive. I am not afraid. Prepare to die."

It giggles. "Me not die."

"Lucy 04, do you copy?"

"Loud and clear. You okay, Doc?"

"I'm fine, but someone coiled at my feet needs a dose of lighter fluid. You got any napes."

"Two on the midline."

"Roll in from my three o'clock, and make sure you don't torch my feet." Fifty yards to my right, an A6 the size of a cat, enters a ten degree dive.

As Lucy 04 approaches the serpent, I call *Pickle* and it releases its deadly cannisters.

"Gotcha, Andy, another crispy critter is no more."

In seconds, the mamba bursts into flame.

Lucy 04 pushes full military power while performing a chandelle to express its satisfaction with its kill.

"Hey, Doc, how'd I do?"

"Perfect, 04. Thanks."

"Lucy 04 to Command. Quack's safe. He's cleared immigration and customs and is returning to the material world."

The tiny aircraft arcs skyward, breaking the sound barrier.

*But an A-6 is subsonic; it can't break the sound barrier.*

Lucy 04 comes back, "This one can...and did."

As it flies out of sight, Lucy 04 makes one final comment, "Shake your ass, Andy. They're waiting for you at the bar."

# CHAPTER 18
# REUNION

A LONE ON AN empty beach, I open my eyes.
*This place is familiar. I think I found the wine bottle here. Was that yesterday afternoon? I'm not sure. I didn't drink that much, but my memory is foggy.*

I don't remember where—or even *if*— I slept, last night. My Parkinson's tremor is low-key at the moment. I'm walking like a normal person; no Parkinson's shuffle.

I look up and down the beach. Not much to see, just the usual seagulls hanging in the wind. I'm not hungry, or thirsty for that matter. The tropical air soothes me with its gentle breeze and mild humidity. The sun is nearing noon. Cumulus clouds build puffy ice cream castles—we're sure to have rain later.

Other than not knowing where I am, I'm content. As I look across the open water, silver flashes of light catch my eye. Then I see what's happening. It's a pod of Spinner Dolphins. I've seen them on YouTube, but this is my first time in real life. Look at them; just like the videos. They must be playing...or chasing something. They repeat their circular tracks, each time coming nearer to shore.

And me without a camera, a phone, or anything. I check my pockets just to be sure. Instead, I find a coin of some sort.

It's a commemorative coin from my old A-6 squadron. I went to Iraq with the Bengals and flew over twenty combat missions there. It turned out to be a short war. Nothing much happened to me. When the war was over, we all went our separate ways and lost track of each other. To tell the truth, I can't remember the last time I've so much as thought about my old squadron.

I flop on the sand to take a closer look at the coin. One side displays the *Eagle, Globe, and Anchor* surrounded by a red ring with the words, *United States Marine Corps* and *Semper Fidelis* stamped on the edge. The reverse bears the squadron insignia, a Bengal Tiger, and the letters, *VMA (AW) 224 - Operation Desert Storm.*

My focus breaks when a red fox runs past me so close I could reach out and touch it. A hundred yards down the beach it stops, looks back, and barks with a high-pitched, yippy sound.

*Is she inviting me to follow?*

I haven't run in a long time, but I'm pretty good at power walking. When I get close, the fox turns and runs ahead. We repeat this routine several times until I hear sounds of people carousing in the distance. When I stop to listen, the fox vanishes.

It's good to hear human voices. Maybe I'll meet some people to hang out with. By the sounds of it, I'm sure there's beer in abundance.

I draw near to an open, roofed structure filled with scores of men my age and a smaller smattering of women. It's basically an outdoor bar with a roof. Everyone appears to be enjoying themselves; drinking, laughing, and cursing aplenty. I was right, frothy beer mugs clutter tables and the floor.

I don't venture too close. If it's a private gathering, I don't want to crash it.

I freeze when a voice calls, "Hey, look everybody, the Quack is back!"

In seconds, I'm engulfed by a bunch of guys slapping my back, shaking my hand, and spilling their beer. Clearly, they know me. That's more than I can say for myself at the moment. They call me Doc, Quack, Andy, or Pete. I don't have to be Einstein to figure out they must be from my former squadron. And specifically those from our Desert Storm deployment.

I reach in my pocket and pull out the coin. "Anybody ever see one of these?"

Laughing hard enough to spill more beer, everyone pulls out the exact same coin. "We made these after returning home from the Middle East. We promised to have it with us anytime we get together."

A voice above the din shouts, "Attention on deck."

Everybody snaps-to, followed by cheers directed at a distinguished, white-haired man who carries himself with pride befitting a Marine officer. Lieutenant Colonel Fox-Golf Carter was our skipper in Desert Storm. We had immense respect for him. Frequently, air crews said if Fox-Golf were flying into hell, they'd volunteer to be his wingman.

With everybody focused on the Skipper, an old unwelcome fear floods my mind and I give in to it. I decide to sneak away...retreat. Too many feelings gushing into my mind; too many memories. I don't think I can take it. Since nobody's paying attention to me, I'll disappear like General MacArthur and simply fade away. If I walk in a westerly direction, nobody will notice because the late-afternoon sun will be shining in their eyes.

As I walk, I gaze at the orange disc hovering a fist-width above the horizon and pay scant attention to a flock of crows passing overhead.

Then, a bright gold flash near the sun seizes my attention. "What the...?"

Then a second flash; this time I literally feel something mechanical click in my brain. In an instant everything becomes clear. I feel strong, confidant . . . *I feel real.* No more evasion or retreat. My memory is open for business. It's not an exaggeration, I feel I've been reborn

I hustle back to the festivities. When I arrive, the party is raging; the stereo playing a Bette Midler tune. I'm finally squared away. I stand erect, shoulders back, and stride forward, leading with my chest.

I walk directly to Fox-Golf. "General, it's good to see you after so many years. Other than your white hair, you look the same as the last time I saw you."

He grabs my left arm and pumps my right hand simultaneously; a handshake fit for real men. "Doc, I'm so glad you could finally make it. We know it's been a long haul for you."

Although I feel confidant, my memory isn't a hundred percent...not yet. "My memory isn't so good, Skipper. How many reunions have we had?"

"Two, roughly one every ten years."

"I know this may sound strange...but, have I attended any?"

He laughs. "C'mon, Doc, you'd remember if you'd been to the others. Our reunions are legendary. Glad you finally made it to this one."

Fox Golf and I are rudely interrupted when a dozen guys crowd in and pepper me with questions. "Where've you been? How's the family? How come we haven't seen you? How long has it been? Are you still practicing?"

They talk so fast, no one waits for an answer. Just as well, my random access memory has yet to reach a gigabyte. I smile, laugh, and nod frequently, pretending to answer their questions. We settle around a table and try to see whether we can drink the last Corona in the place. Of course, that requires matching shots of Cuervo Gold.

"Hey, Doc, remember our last trip to Yuma? Didn't you devour the most nachos at Chretin's before we deployed? How many did you eat?"

"Sixty-nine. My secret was to eat them four at a time, and only when they had just come from the kitchen. If lukewarm, they settle in your stomach like an oil-soaked dishrag."

With continued reminiscing, I remember more and more. Of course, Corona and Jose Cuervo help me remember, as well. I am beginning to remember names.

Nearly sloshed, we start singing *The Halls of Montezuma*. Quality isn't the goal, volume is. Some guys go to the head or grab something from the buffet. Others break into twos and threes and continue regaling each other with *sea stories*.

I'm relaxed and just drunk enough to glow. It's turning dark; the busboys light Tiki torches to illuminate the gathering. More women have joined. I recall several deployed with us, but I'm not sure any were air crew members. Most are wives or girlfriends; wives older, girlfriends younger. I don't see any kids. That makes sense, I'm sure their kids are in their twenties.

One woman, gray-haired, masculine-appearing and over-weight strides directly to me. She's accompanied by a younger, prettier companion. I know I should recognize her; something's familiar in her strength and focus. Psychiatry taught me how to read emotions from faces. Her face reveals three: depression, hope, and gladness.

"Well, Doc, do you recognize me?"

"Memory's foggy. Give me a hint."

She shakes her index finger in my face. "You bring my aircraft back in its current condition or there'll be hell to pay."

"Staff Sergeant Bennett. I'll be damned!"

Her lips tremble and she looks down as if trying to figure out what to say next.

When I place my hand on her shoulder, she wraps her arms around my neck and cries from the depths of her heart. "Oh, dear Doc, did I do something wrong? Did I mess up something in the ejection system? I haven't been able to forgive myself. For years I've tried to sleep but I see you being tortured. It's my fault, I'm so sorry."

Her companion wraps her arms around both of us. "Joyce, I've watched you suffer all these years. Nothing has freed you from this pain."

Turning her face to me the young woman pleads. "Doc, you're our last hope. Joyce and I married twelve years ago. I hoped my love was strong enough for both of us, but she's never healed."

In the center of my heart, a golden light grows. I feel warm, abundant, and loving, but also with the certainty this is my calling. Jesse flashes before my eyes, "Well done, Peter. It's time for your calling."

The golden lights flows from my body. Its purpose: wrap Joyce and her wife in the golden light. Hold them until they become gold too. When I see them totally gold, a gold raven takes them and they float toward heaven.

At the same time our bodies remain entwined. A moment of silence passes until Joyce draws back. "What happened? I f-feel free, light as a whisper."

She turns to her companion. "Mia...I . . ."

"Don't say more, Joyce. I know something just happened. Didn't a golden bird fly away with us? But yet, we're still here...everything *feels* new."

The couple embraces until Mia looks at me. "Did we just experience a miracle?"

"You just experienced a healing."

"How did you do that?"

"I'm new at this. I can't explain it yet. I do know Joyce's mind was tied in an impenetrable knot. I helped you untie it. It's a gift I developed since my own healing."

"How long ago did that happen?"

"About an hour."

My tremor reminds me my PD hasn't disappeared. No worries. Doesn't every neurologist remind us PD is incurable. I have developed some ideas that don't completely agree with that.

Fox-Golf comes over and sits next to me. "Even though we haven't spoken since Iraq, I've followed your life from a distance. I can't imagine how hard it's been. Besides everything else, you got Parkinson's disease. How's it coming along?"

"I pretty-much manage it by engaging my mind and avoiding meds."

"How many years has it been?"

"Depends on how you count the years. It's been nine since my tremor started."

"That's pretty unusual, isn't it. I mean going that long without medicine. My father-in-law had it. After a few years he could hardly get around; blamed it on the disease and too many meds."

He leans back and folds his arms. "Your bigger battle has been the aftermath of getting shot down. Yours was the only aircraft we lost."

"My memory is still pretty sketchy about the whole affair, but it's coming back. One thing I haven't understood is why Pudge never reached out to me."

The General stiffens and places his beer on the table. He stares for a moment at the empty mug. Finally, he looks at me. "Pudge never made it home in spite of your heroic efforts."

"Would you repeat that? I don't think I heard you right."

"Pudge didn't make it. His spinal cord was severed during the ejection."

My brain app jumps to warp speed. "I...I thought he was okay. Are you sure?"

"I saw his body."

My first impulse is to launch into non-stop retching. For a second, I feel like I might lose it. But before I get very far, my inner glow reminds me things have changed.

Fox Golf gives me time to collect myself. "I arrived overhead the same time the choppers. Those Sea Cobras were killing sons-of-bitches. We were prepared to press the attack, but quit when the choppers said there were two of our guys down there. I flew lower, but I couldn't see you.

"Do you know what happened to Pudge?"

"When we debriefed that night, the chopper medics said they found you standing over Pudge's body and holding an empty AK-47. There were seven enemy dead. Further away, they found another dozen bodies near your torso harness. But something we never figured out was why several had their throats cut and the rest were shot."

*Stay focused, Peter, you're in charge*

"So, Pudge died."

"Yeah, but he died because he hit the ground too hard. The aircraft was in a tight turn when you ejected. Your Martin-Baker seats shot you parallel to the ground. Neither of your chutes fully deployed."

"Do you know if he died then?"

"He died just after he arrived back at the base."

My CO places a hand on my shoulder. "Something else you should know; there was no sign any enemy ever laid a hand on him. You protected him to the end."

I lean back and become aware of how quiet the room has become. Most of the squadron has gathered around—some kneeling, some standing. I look up and scan the group. All I see are men's faces expressing respect and a few tears.

I'm feeling something I don't recall since the War. I feel content.

Moments later, I feel another tap on my shoulder. I turn to see an attractive woman that is maybe ten years younger than me. She is petite, has a dazzling white smile, and a rich auburn ponytail. "Mind if I join you, doctor?"

"Not at all. Please come, sit. And please don't call me doctor."

"All my life I've been waiting to meet you. I'm Pudge Cummings' sister. He said you guys had a lot of fun together; drinking and dropping bombs. After he died and I heard about your heroism; I couldn't wait to meet you. But then there were all the years you cut yourself off from the world. I haven't been to a 224 reunion before. But when I heard you might be here; I wouldn't miss it.

*There's something familiar about her. Is it her muscular petite body? Her smile? The way her eyes linger on me?*

"I recall talking to Pudge about you on our last mission. Didn't your husband die about the same time?"

"Yes, he died of cancer."

"Do you have any kids?"

"Two grown sons. But they're always busy."

"I can relate. I hear from my sons every Christmas and on my birthday—whether I need it or not." We say nothing more. We understand...apparently both of us know what it's like to be ignored by our children.

"Did you remarry?"

"I waited for five years before I fell in love with a great guy. I was prepared for some happy-ever-after time, but it became complicated when I developed ovarian cancer the month after we married. Four years of chemo and radiation left me withered and sterile. What finally killed the cancer was immunotherapy."

"Based on how you look today, I think you finally licked it. How did your husband take it?"

She leans back, inspecting her fingernails. "Maybe I'm sharing more than I should, but he divorced me. It wasn't because of fighting or infidelity; he couldn't face the prospect of never having sex for the rest of his life and he would never stoop to having an affair. We actually parted on pretty good terms."

As I listen, a different *something* starts warming my heart. Her words seem to caress me. They feel like waves lapping on a tropical beach. It's not *what* she says as much as *how* she says it. Her voice is kind—*gentle on my mind*.

Focused on what I'm feeling, I continue with casual talk. "Are you in a relationship now?"

"No. And that's not a good thing. Truth is, I'm pretty lonely. But I'm a writer and spend a lot of time with my imagination."

I think I detect some growing hesitancy in her speech. "What do you write?"

"My heart wants to write fiction, but to pay the bills, I am a communications director for a high tech company. I'm lucky, I get to work from home most of the time."

I want to continue talking with this unique woman. "Can I get something for us to drink besides beer?"

"Is it okay if I call you Peter? Everybody calls you Doc or Quack."

"I prefer you call me Peter."

She has a mischievous look in her eye. "How would you like to chat over an obscenely expensive bottle of wine?"

"I would like that, but at the moment I have no money with me."

"Well, I happen to have a bit of cash, and I'm really enjoying our conversation. Would you mind if I buy the wine?"

"I'm a liberated man. I'll let a beautiful woman buy me expensive wine anytime."

"Let's call it *a glad-to-meet-you* libation?"

"That would be great, thanks." I wink. "I'll pay you back at the next reunion."

We part laughing. A couple minutes later, she returns with crystal wineglasses and a bottle of Dom Perignon.

"Wow. I can't recall the last time I drank anything this good. Must have been sometime before Annie died."

"Tell me more about your life, Peter—that is, if you want to."

"To tell the truth, I don't want to go over my life story now. Maybe when we become better friends, I will."

"That's all right with me. I think I know pretty much about your life after the war. Colonel Carter and I made sure you'd never be forgotten"

She touches my hand while reaching to refill my glass.

*Was that an accident or is she beginning to have the same feelings I do?*

I don't withdraw my hand. Rather, I take her hand in mine and gaze into her eyes. She responds with a little squeeze of my hand.

We continue to talk, but our real communication is mind-to-mind, heart-to-heart. Paying no attention to the passage of time, we immerse ourselves in each other.

We break our mind-meld when the cleanup crew asks us to move so they can finish sweeping the floor.

"Peter, where are you staying? I have a rental car. I can give you a ride."

"This is embarrassing. I don't have a place to stay *and* I don't have a car."

She furrows her brow and then reassures me, "I don't need to know why."

I study my shoes before looking up. "Worse, I don't know where I am."

"I know about your mental health challenges. Say no more. Come with me. You can stay with me in my room."

"I would like that. But I don't even know your name."

"My name is Holly."

# AUTHOR'S PHOTOS

MARINE ALL WEATHER ATTACK SQUADRON
224. YUMA, ARIZONA, LATE 1969. PRIOR TO
DEPLOYMENT TO VIETNAM. I AM SIXTH
FROM THE LEFT, FRONT ROW.

PETER ANDRESEN, PRIVATE U.S. ARMY,
BORN 1899, DIED IN FRANCE, 1918
MY MOTHER'S FAVORITE BROTHER
SHE WEPT FOR HIM EVERY MEMORIAL DAY

Made in the USA
Middletown, DE
18 February 2022

61356489R00111